# A Sugar Pine Christmas

## SINGLE DADS ALL THE WAY

### A.D. ELLIS

## ONE

# Mattie Blackwell

"WHO ARE YOU?" the blond kid asked as I hefted a box up the steps of the duplex. Being back in Sugar Pine was surreal, but at least I'd found a nice place to lick my wounds and settle back into my hometown.

The house was a two-story blue-green color. Steps from the sidewalk rose up to meet with three steps to the porch. The porch boasted a white railing, a swing, and two windows in the middle flanked on each far side by a door.

I placed the box on the porch swing and wiped my hands on my jeans. The Midwestern fall season hadn't given up just yet, but a wintery chill danced on the air in promise of freezing temperatures to come.

When I thought I'd make it big in California, the gorgeous weather was one of the biggest draws. Along with escaping the town I'd grown up in and the guy who didn't want me. But now, the thought of a real Sugar Pine winter had excitement coursing through me.

"Who are you?" I asked back with an easy smile. I liked kids. Didn't want any myself, but I enjoyed giving them art lessons. Some of my friends had kids spanning from babies to teens, and I'd always been deemed *good* with them. Probably because I could hand them back to their parents when things got real.

The kid looked to be about thirteen or fourteen. Maybe eighth or ninth grade. Middle-schoolers were a *tough* crowd, but once you found your in with them, you were golden.

He crossed his arms over his chest and jutted out his chin. "Sam!" he hollered over his shoulder. "There's a man out here. He might be a creep."

"What? No," I started, but then I froze.

Sam?

No way in hell.

The door on the other side of the duplex opened, and fourteen years of moving on flashed in front of my eyes before crashing to a screeching halt.

Sam fucking Benton.

It wasn't like I'd thought he'd moved away from Sugar Pine, but I also hadn't truly thought he'd still be here.

Or at least I hadn't let myself think about what it would mean if he was still here.

The worst part? The self-preservation side of me should have screamed at me to grab the box and run far,

far away. Back to California, or maybe I'd give the East Coast a try. What about Oregon? Washington state? I'd heard they were lovely.

But I clearly had no self-preservation side because the only thing my dumb-ass mind could think of was how badly I wanted Sam back then.

And how damn *fine* he still looked now.

Fuck.

We'd both aged, but Sam wore it *very* well. His brown hair showed more silver. There were fourteen years of laugh lines. But his dark brown eyes still sent heat through me.

"Mattie?" Sam asked as he slipped dark-rimmed glasses to rest on the top of his head.

"Sam."

In two long strides, Sam was across the porch pulling me into a hug. He smelled like home, and he felt even better.

"You two know each other?" the kid asked, arms still crossed, standing beside us glancing back and forth like a spectator at a tennis match.

"This is my friend, Mattie. He ran off back before you were born." The edge in Sam's voice offered just enough challenge for me to remember why I'd been so gone for this man.

We'd both come to Sugar Pine about the same time. Me returning from getting my art degree. Sam moving to town to be closer to his twin sister who, at that time, was stationed at a somewhat nearby Air Force base.

Sam and I had struck up an easy friendship, both of us living and working in the small town. Most friends my age had moved away when we finished college. Those who'd stayed were married and having kids. Sam was easy to talk to, and we spent many lunches chatting at the diner.

Evenings at the Sugar Pine Tap were spent sipping beers, laughing, and watching idiots fight over pool games.

And then, two years into our friendship, things changed.

I pushed the thoughts away and turned toward the kid. "I'm Mattie Blackwell. I used to live in Sugar Pine. You must be Tabitha's son?"

He narrowed his eyes and threw a glance toward Sam. When the older man nodded, the kid stuck out his hand. "I'm Toby Benton. You know my mom?"

"I do. And I think she's got a shit load of explaining to do."

When I'd talked to my old friend Tabitha Benton, I'd forced myself to push the fact that she was Sam's twin sister out of my mind. She said she had a perfect half of a duplex to rent to me, and I didn't question it. I knew she was now a Major in the Air Force and did something with flying heavy aircraft when she was deployed, but I also knew she owned several properties in Sugar Pine and the surrounding towns.

Four towns butted up against each other in a tidy little square in Evergreen County—Sugar Pine, Red

Pine, White Pine, and Jack Pine were all similar Midwestern towns, each vying to bring in the most tourism with their quaint festivals throughout the year, gorgeous scenery, and their namesake Christmas tree decorated on the town square each holiday season— although, not all of the pine types made great holiday décor.

All four had been settled at the same time and, since they were in the same geographic location, it was hard to tell a difference between them as Pine River split into four forks in the northwest corner of Evergreen County and ran right through each.

It was fun to visit each town to see the namesake pines growing and learn fun facts about them. All the trees were native, but the early folks had taken it upon themselves to plant more of one type in each town.

I was biased, but I thought Sugar Pine had the most interesting fact; when the town was originally settled, there was an argument about the type of trees they were planting. An older brother swore it was a Pitch Pine while the younger brother argued it was a Sugar Pine. The younger brother ended up dying in a hunting accident. Even though the older brother still swore the trees they planted were Pitch Pines, he honored his deceased brother by naming the town Sugar Pine.

Years later, it would be declared the trees they'd planted were indeed Pitch Pines, but everyone agreed Sugar Pine was a better name, so it stuck.

Along with their histories and fun facts, each town

had its own festivals, food specialties, and claims to the most picturesque backdrops through every season.

But Sugar Pine was home, and it was the first place I wanted to be when I finally admitted California wasn't for me.

Tabitha having a place for me was like fate.

But I should have questioned it.

*Really* should have questioned it.

Shit.

"She's not here," Toby said. "Gone for nine months."

"Nine months?" I glanced toward Sam, and he nodded.

"Tabby and I live together," he said. "She goes on deployment for six to twelve months. While she's gone, I'm Super Uncle-Slash-Dad Extraordinaire."

Toby snorted and rolled his eyes, but it was in good fun.

"When she's home for the same amount of time, I take a backseat and let her be Mom of the Year." He shrugged. "Been doing it since this one was born. It works for us."

I glanced toward the door that was supposed to be my side of the duplex. "And you live on the other side?"

"We do. Moved in when Tabby got pregnant and moved to Sugar Pine; my apartment wasn't gonna cut it." Sam ran a hand down his face and scratched at the brown and silver scruff on his jawline. "I should have wondered why she was so vague about the new renter."

I sighed. "Is this going to be okay?" I didn't want to get into too much history in front of Toby.

I'd paid the first and last month's rent. Tabby had sent pictures of the den I was going to use as a studio, and the basement where I'd be able to store my art supplies. I *really* liked the house.

Sam smiled easily. He'd always had an easy smile. "It's fine. We'll enjoy having a decent neighbor."

"Do you smoke crack?" Toby asked, his eyes narrowed.

"What? No." I scowled.

"The last guy smoked crack. We kicked him out. The people before that were nice, but they moved to Denver. Do you have kids? No one ever has kids my age. One guy had a big ol' dog he let me play with." Toby turned to Sam. "Can we have pizza rolls for lunch?"

Sam chuckled. "You can fix some in the air fryer as a snack. I'll fix something a little healthier for lunch."

Toby rushed into the house. "Bye, Mattie."

Then it was just Sam and me.

"It's really fine," Sam said. "Tabitha is probably laughing her ass off—she never did give up on the idea of you and me together."

I forced a smile. "Yeah, well, we both know how that played out. I'll give her shit, but this place is way too nice to turn down."

"It's good to have you home," Sam said. I'd forgotten how genuine he could be.

My heart thumped double-time with memories of the past—good and bad.

Home.

I was home.

Not going to lie, I *really* liked the idea of living so near to Sam.

Shit.

Yesterday, if you'd asked me about my past with Sam Benton, I would have scoffed it off as a momentary lack of judgment.

Immaturity.

A passing phase where I found myself hot for a man I considered a friend.

Wanting something I couldn't have.

Nothing more.

But now?

Well, *now* had me face-to-face with my past, and every cell in my body rejoiced.

Moving on hadn't worked well at all it seemed.

Maybe I was a glutton for punishment, but seeing Sam brought back every single memory. Sure, it was unrequited back then, and probably now, but that didn't mean my dumb ass wasn't going to fall right back into being hot and bothered by the man.

We'd been friends back then.

We hadn't ended on *bad* terms, just realistic ones.

Sam and I were nearing forty now. We'd lived a lot of life since then. Surely, we could be pleasant neighbors. Maybe even rekindle the friendship.

*Like friendship is all you want.*

Yeah, well.

Unless things had changed drastically over the years, Sam wasn't interested.

I'd just have to admire from afar.

I was an artist. Pain and suffering fueled my work.

Looked like I'd have plenty of it.

I hoped my clients were ready for lots of longing desire and pining in my upcoming works.

But I was home in Sugar Pine to create new pieces, tackle the new job I'd taken on, and spend Christmas in my hometown for the first time in fourteen years.

Anything with Sam would just be icing on the cake.

TWO

## Sam Denton

"*WE BOTH KNOW how that played out.*"

Mattie's words played over and over in my head as I waited for the mayor of Sugar Pine to show up for our appointment.

Mattie looked damn good fourteen years ago, and he looked even better now.

He'd somehow grown into himself.

God, it seemed like a lifetime ago that he left Sugar Pine, but seeing him on the porch talking to my nephew brought the past back like a fist to the face.

Fourteen years was long enough the man should have been out of my head.

Just a glimmer of memory in my heart.

Instead, he'd always been the one who got away when I allowed myself to think about him.

*And whose fault was that?*

I did regret how things played out, but life had

kicked into hyper-speed back then, and I really hadn't known how to deal with so much happening at once.

We'd met when we were somewhere along the line of twenty-two or twenty-three. Not exactly founts of knowledge and years of experience.

I'd just gotten out of school, was working as a web designer, missing my sister, and living in a new town. Becoming friends with Mattie had been easy and fulfilling. We had a couple great years of hanging out and keeping each other sane in Sugar Pine.

Then my sister got pregnant, and the father fucked right off to go back to his wife and three children. The only saving grace was he wasn't in the Air Force, so she didn't have to be worried about seeing him around.

Right as Tabitha and I were deciding to live together in Sugar Pine so I could help when the baby came along, Mattie and I hit a snag in our friendship.

Not a *snag* really.

Just a realization and a possible new direction.

But Mattie's realization had only been about his feelings for me in particular.

He was more than ready to strike out in a new direction. His creative spirit and willingness to throw himself into something new were some of the things that drew me to him.

However, *my* realization hit a lot harder because admitting I had feelings for Mattie was a uniquely new experience for me. Being attracted to a man for the first time at the age of twenty-five meant I spent a lot of time thinking.

And overthinking.

And then thinking through it some more.

Add to the situation that my sister had just found out she was going to be a single mother while serving in the Air Force.

Mattie was ready to move wherever his creative soul whispered for him to go.

And he wanted me to leave Sugar Pine with him.

*Boom.*

Overload.

So, yeah. Mattie wasn't wrong with his comment about how things played out.

But he wasn't completely right either.

It wasn't because I didn't share in his feelings of wanting to explore the spark between us. But back then, it had been easier to let him chase after his dream while I stayed back to help Tabitha. Sure, I eventually allowed the word *gay* into my thoughts and finally told my sister, but it had taken a long couple years thanks to our upbringing.

Tabitha and I only had each other and crappy memories from our childhood, but our past held a lot of conditioning we had to work through.

Admitting I was gay was a turning point in my life—something that needed to happen so I could truly embrace the real me. It wasn't like I came out and immediately started looking for *the one*, but it had been freeing and allowed me to figure a lot of shit out. Since then, I'd done my fair share of short-term relationships, but none of them had stuck.

Guys didn't like the set-up Tabitha and I had.

Or they didn't want a guy who was a single dad for long chunks of time, and an involved uncle the rest of the time.

Or they weren't a fan of kids.

Mostly it was a combination of all three.

Toby was my first priority, and any man I maybe wanted to start something with had to understand that from the get-go.

Watching Mattie interact so easily with Toby on that first day did funny things to my gut. If I was being honest, coming face-to-face with the man had sent my head into a spiral of what-ifs and second chances.

Was Mattie willing to forgive me and move beyond the past?

According to Tabby—I'd given her an earful when she called to talk to Toby, but she'd just laughed—I needed to just be honest with Mattie and see where things might go.

What did she know?

Mattie had been in the duplex a couple days now, and we'd had a few superficial chats. The pull toward him was just as strong as it was back then, but I wasn't sure where we stood. Could we jump right back into the friendship and attraction? Or were we so different after all these years that we'd need to get to know each other all over again?

Toby was definitely interested in the artist living next door.

My nephew was a great kid. Definitely entering those teenage years—which scared the fuck out of me because I had no clue what to do with a teen...not that I'd had any idea what to do with an infant, a toddler, a child, or a preteen—but he did well at school for the most part and didn't cause too many problems.

He had a few friends at school, and they would hang out at the park or playing video games online. Luckily, Toby's game room was in the basement so the yelling he liked to do on the headset was mostly muted.

I thought we had a pretty decent relationship, but each time his mom got deployed, and we faced up to a year on our own, I worried it would be the year he decided he hated having his mom gone so much and his gay uncle struggling through being a stand-in father.

Toby, who huffed and groaned about having to do the dishes, clean his room, or gather the trash, had voluntarily helped Mattie carry in load after load and tear down boxes once he'd fueled up on pizza rolls.

The gut punch of emotions that brought me was surprising, but I was happy to see my nephew taking initiative, being kind, and finding a good man to look up to.

Sure, he had me, but I knew I'd pretty much lost the

chance to be the cool guncle about the same time I'd agreed to play pseudo-father to help my sister.

Tabitha and I had found an online parenting forum when Toby was an infant—it supplemented the books and articles we read while trying to quell the anxiety over the impending arrival of a tiny human.

The forum had a ton of information—to the point of being overwhelming if you let it—but it was very useful. After sifting through the shit-ton of categories and subgroups, I'd found one specifically for single fathers, and they'd helped me through every stage of my nephew's life so far.

In fact, I'd already logged in to pose the question about Toby latching on to Mattie so quickly.

**Uncle Sam**: *A friend from my past is back in town. T. looks at him like he walks on water. Don't get me wrong, he's a great guy and I have no problems with T. looking up to him. I guess I'm just feeling a little left out. I can't get him to wash the dishes or pick up his wet towel, but he's tripping over himself to do physical labor for the new neighbor.*

The response from one of the other dads wasn't an answer, but my post hadn't really indicated it was a problem. Overall, the reply from Dad I am helped to ease some of my irritation. I decided I had to be happy Toby thought the sun rose and set on Mattie instead of someone I didn't like and respect.

**Dad I am**: *I feel where you're coming from. I used to be close with my son, but once we hit the teenage years things have been touchy. It's all part of being a teenager, I guess. They want to live their own lives and find new heroes to look up to.*

Sighing and checking my watch, I shifted in my chair. Annoyed by the mayor's tardiness and feeling out of sorts over Mattie being back in town, I wished for the meeting to get started sooner rather than later so I could get home and finish up some work before starting the weekend.

The door to the reception area burst open and Mayor Darcy Joseph blew in. He was a tiny man with huge dark-rimmed glasses, a little Pooh belly, and the most southern Midwestern accent I'd ever heard. Everyone knew he'd been born and raised in Sugar Pine, but his paternal grandmother was from the deep south, and she lived with his family from the time of his birth until her death several years ago. He laughed that she taught him how to make sweet tea, knit a shawl, bless someone's heart, and speak like a Southern Belle.

"Sam, my deepest apologies, dear. I bustled my little bottom to the coffee shop for a cup of Annie's piping hot sweet tea with a splash of cream just the way I like it." He paused with a hand on his chest as he caught his breath. "Well, everyone who is anyone was at One Lump or Two, so the line was just atrocious. Now, I don't like to flaunt my position, so I got in line like everyone else. But then dear ol' Missus Baker fell right out on the floor. Of course, I had to wait until the emergency crew arrived *and* direct traffic while a group of good Samaritans caught Mr. Pookie." He took another deep breath. "In all the excitement, I missed out on ordering my tea *and* lost track of time. What a mess of a morning, please forgive me, dear." Pushing his glasses up his nose he leaned on his administrative assistant's desk. "Pammy, would you be an absolute dear and brew me a cup of tea? Strong, sweet, and splash of cream if you'd be so kind." He finally straightened his clothing and turned back to me. "Shall we?"

Pulling myself from the trance his little one-man spiel about Missus Baker and her Pomeranian had thrown me into, I stood and joined him by his office door. He barely reached my shoulder, but I was used to many people being shorter than my six-foot-two frame.

Mattie was slightly taller than me.

No.

Nope.

Not the time to think about Mattie.

No matter how good he looked in his worn jeans and flannel as he hefted boxes into his new home.

"It's so good to see you," Darcy started as we entered his office. "How's Tobias? Tabitha?"

"They're good, thanks. Tabby has about six more months until she's home." I took a seat as Darcy scuttled to settle himself behind his desk.

"Such a strain on your family; her service is so appreciated." He clicked a few things on his computer as he spoke. "How's business? Keeping you busy?"

I chuckled. The good thing about web design was I could work from anywhere. Technology allowed me to meet with clients from across the world, although the majority of my work was with individuals and businesses in the States. "Business is good. I like to stay busy."

"Good, good," he said absently as he scribbled something on a notebook. "Sam, I brought you here today because I'm in need of your services. Well, Sugar Pine is."

I cocked a brow. I'd done some work for the Evergreen County Library, the Sugar Pine grocery store, a used car lot in Jack Pine, and the county fair along with a couple individuals in Sugar Pine and neighboring towns. But most of my work was spread out across the country and even across oceans. "I'm listening."

"Sam, when I took over as mayor of Sugar Pine, I falsely believed our people, food, and nature would be enough to sell our location to the tourists." Darcy sighed as he stood and moved to the window. "Over time, I've realized that we *must* do more if we're to be the top town in Evergreen County. The website is sorely lacking—"

"We have a website?"

"Exactly." He tutted around his office watering various plants as he spoke. "Of course, I want a professional to work on this job, but keeping it local is important too."

My gut told me the next words out of his mouth were going to be about money. It was always about money.

"Now, Sam, we'd pay you, of course," Darcy said. "I wouldn't expect you to work for free." He gave a hearty chortle. "Not going to argue if you want to offer a discount, though."

There it was.

"Anyway," he waved away the comment before I could reply, "I also want new artwork around town, as well as featured on the website. I've brought in another local; I think the two of you will make a fabulous team."

As if planned, a knock sounded at the door.

"Ah, there he is now. Come in."

The door swung open, and Mattie blew into the room like sunshine. Back then, things always seemed better when he was around. And now, it seemed not much had changed. How did everything feel softer, lighter, and more enjoyable just because this gorgeous man had walked in?

Mattie was the personification of *He lights up a room*, and there was no better way to describe him. Intense, emotional, and displaying a tendency to pour his feelings into his work, but also so easy-going and fun.

"Mattie Brightwell, I'd like you to meet Sam Benton." Darcy gestured between us. "Sam, this is

Mattie. He's an artist. A Sugar Pine boy through and through."

Not being one to skip manners, I stood and held out my hand with a smile. "Mattie."

His lips quirked, and he yanked me into a back-slapping hug. "Sam, you don't look a day over thirty-nine. How you doin', man?"

I let his warmth spill over me, the clean, fresh scent of his skin tickling my nostrils, and hugged him back.

"Well, I'll be," Darcy exclaimed. "Do you boys know each other?"

I couldn't tell from the sparkle in the old man's eyes if he was just truly pleased with the surprise or if he'd known about me and Mattie before and was just playing innocent.

Either way, I wasn't upset to have a reason to be talking to Mattie.

"We go way back," Mattie said, squeezing my arm. "Mayor, I would have been excited about the chance to spruce up Sugar Pine anyway, but knowing you want Sam and me to work together makes it all the better."

"Good, good. Well, this is just perfect." Darcy launched into his wants and wishes for the website. "It needs to be user-friendly and really give the vibe of Sugar Pine. We have someone on staff in charge of advertising, so don't worry about any of that. You boys will just be in charge of making it look nice." He jotted something in his notebook. "Mattie, when we spoke, you indicated you could provide us some good prices on your paintings and photographs to hang around town."

Mattie nodded. "Sure can."

"We'll likely want something in the main businesses and definitely in the cabins down by Pine River. The lodge too." He clasped his hands in front of him. "Now, I can pass this along to someone else, but Mattie is a hometown boy, and Sam might as well be since he's been here so long, so I thought I'd put it to you boys first."

Mattie's eyes shone bright, and he waggled his brows in my direction.

"Our summer and fall seasons bring in the most tourism with camping and hiking. Spring can be wet and cold, but folks like to hit the trails and water as soon as we get a few warm days. The winter season used to be a lucrative time, but tourism is down." Darcy turned his computer screen our way and pointed to it. "There's a grant being offered to a struggling small town. Now, I don't like to admit we're struggling, but that grant money sure would come in handy."

"What's the requirement?" Mattie asked.

"We have to pull in the largest percentage of income compared to the same time period last year, have a fresh, new website, and involve locals in making it all happen."

"Deadline?" I asked.

"Christmas Eve."

The matching grunts of surprise escaping Mattie and me had Darcy holding up a placating hand. "I know it's not much time, but I think it can be done. Mattie, the pieces don't have to be new or one-of-a-kind. You mentioned you had some pieces you'd had printed in multiples, those would be just fine. Sam, we have an existing website, so you're not starting from scratch—however, if it would be easier to do so, you have cart blanche with that, obviously. What we really need is something to draw folks to Sugar Pine in the winter. The trails are great year-round, but that goes for all four towns in the county. Most of our big festivals are in the summer and fall. Jack Pine and Red Pine lucked out with the higher hills for skiing, although we pull in our fair share with the sledding hills for families of all ages." He tapped a finger against his lips. "You're both creatives in your own right. We *need* something that can grow year to year and continually pull people in. I'm not trying to steal tourists right out from the other Pines' noses, that's just not very hospitable. But my mind sees tourists coming to stay in the White Pine Hotel or our little cabins and spending their days visiting all the grand things to do in each town. Right now, I'm not sure Sugar Pine has that big draw, and that's what I'm counting on you boys for."

The meeting wrapped up, and Darcy had us meet with Pam to sign contracts regarding dates, pay, and requirements of the job. Then Mattie and I were out on the sidewalk in the late fall sunshine.

"Wanna get lunch and brainstorm since we're colleagues for a while?" I asked.

Mattie smiled, a million megawatts sending unfamiliar flutters to my chest. "Absolutely. And maybe you can tell me why you've been avoiding me."

## THREE
### *Mattie*

"AVOIDING YOU?" Sam's brow furrowed, but a flash of guilt crossed his gorgeous face.

I quirked a brow.

He sighed. "I don't know," he started as we headed toward the Sugar Pine diner. "I'm happy you're back home, but I don't know how to just pick right back up where we left off."

I snorted. "Well, if we're picking right back up where we left off, that would mean me making an ass of myself by kissing you, so it's probably okay to skip that part."

Sam huffed. "Yeah, I'd rather not revisit the mess of fourteen years ago."

Now it was my turn to sigh. "Sorry to bring the mess right back to your doorstep."

"What? No, I didn't mean you. My life has changed a lot since then, and I really don't want to go back to all that uncertainty."

I wasn't sure if he was talking about our friendship or Toby or something else, so I opted to steer clear for now. "Well, before I fucked things up and left, we had a pretty good thing, so maybe we start back there?"

Sam cocked his head, his eyes meeting mine as he held the door open for me. He didn't speak until we were seated, as luck would have it at our *usual* table, and glancing over the menus.

"You didn't fuck things up," he mumbled, not looking up from the laminated menu.

"Huh?"

He took a deep breath. "You didn't fuck things up. Things were messy back then with Tabby and the baby coming. I missed you when you left, but we both had things we needed to do."

"Well, I'm sorry I put you in an uncomfortable situation. I let feelings get the best of me and didn't stop to think." I shrugged. "Moving to California was good and bad for me, but I don't regret it. Just glad to be home."

Just when Sam looked as if he wanted to say something else, the waitperson arrived to take our orders.

I couldn't help but smile as Sam ordered the Frisco melt and fries, and I ordered the BLT with cottage cheese. When his eyes met mine, it was like we were transported back fourteen years ago and ordering our lunches to share like usual.

"So, I guess we need a plan for how we're going to mesh our projects and get that grant," I said, sipping my unsweet tea.

Sam huffed. "I need to take a look at the website and decide if it's going to be easier to update or just scrap it and start over. Do you have enough artwork to fill what Darcy wants?"

I nodded. "Pretty much. I may need to paint a few quickies, but most of my photography series are already framed and ready to hang."

"Make sure you get a fair price for them," Sam warned.

"I will. The paintings are old ones that never sold or ones I just did for fun. The photographs are a series combining trees, flowers, and the Pine River from way back. I do have a series of interesting buildings along with a set of beach pictures from California. I think those will mostly be enough. I just need to finish up framing a few of them."

"You frame your own now?" Sam asked.

"Yep. Finally got tired of trying to find someone to do it for me—it got even more expensive when I hit the west coast. So, I learned how to do it myself."

"That adds to the value, right?"

I shrugged. "I add to the cost so I'm not losing money, but I don't know about the *value*."

"Still underestimating yourself? Shame on you." He pretended to scold me over the same argument we'd had countless times.

Our food arrived and, as if muscle memory kicked in, he handed me half his sandwich at the same time I held out half of my BLT.

Grabbing a fry from his plate, I grinned broadly.

Sam jabbed my hand with a fork before scooping up a bite of cottage cheese.

Just like that, the friendship was back on track.

And the sharpness in my heart was simply due to my happiness at having my friend back. That mixture of pleasure and pain had nothing to do with how badly I still wanted him.

How much I wanted to press into him and devour his mouth.

Our friendship was good back then, and it could be good now.

I just had to accept that Sam didn't see me the same way I saw him.

Hell, for all I knew, he had a girlfriend. I'd need to get myself mentally and emotionally prepared to meet her.

The BLT was sawdust on my tongue, but I pressed on. "Sugar Pines aren't the best for Christmas trees, but neither are Jack or Red Pines. White Pines are probably the best for decorating, so I think we're better off to not focus on the Christmas tree angle."

"Agreed. Each town already does unique decorations on their namesake tree, so that's probably out," Sam said. "I think we need to take a look at your work, figure out where the pieces are going to be displayed, and work together to get some of your work onto the website. Then we can get some focus on the site with everything the town has to offer."

"Damn, you've given this some thought."

Sam scoffed. "Don't act like you haven't. You already know the pieces you want to use, and you've been thinking about how we can draw people in."

We smirked and ate our lunch in silence for a bit.

"I think it would be best if we take in the town like tourists. Make some notes, take some pictures, really home in on what we want to feature," Sam said, but then his cheeks pinked. "If you're down for that. If not, I can do that part myself."

"No," I answered, probably much too quickly. "That sounds good. What if we ask Toby for ideas too? But we need to work quickly if we're going to meet that deadline."

Sam smiled like a proud father when I mentioned Toby. "He'd love that. Probably wouldn't admit it—at least not to me—but he'll get a kick out of being involved. And he's smart, a thinker, he'll probably have good ideas."

I cocked my head. "You used to say you didn't think you wanted kids."

Sam's eyes met mine and a cloudy look crossed his face, but it was gone quickly. "I didn't want to fuck up a kid. Tabby and I pretty much watched our parents suck at life. I figured that was all I knew, and I'd never be able to keep a relationship going thanks to them. Didn't want to pass that on to a kid." He shrugged, a faraway look in his eyes. "But then Tabby got pregnant. She's a huge advocate for women's rights—especially with her position as a female in the military—but abortion wasn't something she wanted at that point in her life. She hadn't planned on Toby, but she wanted him."

"You did a really good thing by stepping up for her."

He shook his head. "There was no choice. She's my twin sister. Most of our life we only had each other. There was no way I could leave her to raise Toby on her own."

"And you like it?" I asked. "Being a father?"

Sam took a deep breath. "That's a loaded question."

"You don't have to tell me."

He swirled a fry in ketchup. "Being a parent is *hard*. Sometimes I wish I could just be the fun uncle, but when it's just Toby and me, I have to wear the dad shoes."

"He seems like a great kid. Helpful, polite, responsible. I've enjoyed having him around these last few days."

"Pretty sure he's never looked at me the way he looks at you. You're like larger than life in his eyes," Sam said.

"It's always easier to be in awe of someone if it's not your parent. Coaches, teachers, neighbors, uncles, friends' parents. I remember *all* those people being cooler than my own parents."

"Yeah, I get it. Tabby and I have this online parenting forum we read and post questions on. There's a single dad's group that's been really helpful. They said the same thing." Sam's bright eyes met mine. "If he has to think someone else is cooler than me, I'm glad it's you."

I struggled to swallow my last bite of Frisco melt around the lump in my throat. "Well, I remember what it's like to be a teenager. I wasn't sure if coming back home was for the best, but if it means getting to hang out with you *and* getting to know Toby, I'm all for it."

The bell over the door jingled reminding me of Christmas. Maybe coming home to Sugar Pine, to Sam and Toby, would end up being the best decision I ever made.

FOUR

*Sam*

"WHY DO YOU LOOK LIKE THAT?" Toby asked.

"Like what?" I stopped pacing and wiped my hands on my jeans before recognizing the nervous movement and shoving my hands in my pockets.

Toby gave me a *duh* look. "Like *that*. Like you're all nervous."

"Not nervous. Mattie's coming over and we're going to work on the grant project." I'd explained the job to Toby and told him to give some thought to ways we could get families to want to come to Sugar Pine around the holidays.

My nephew crossed his arms and narrowed his eyes. "But you're like sweaty and weird."

I scoffed. "I'm not...I'm just ready to get the job...it's not like—" My words stalled out.

"Oh my god, do you *like* him?" Toby's voice held

that perfect teen mixture of disgust, incredulity, and humor.

"What? No...I mean..." I sighed and pinched the bridge of my nose. "Yes? I don't know."

Toby rolled his eyes. "Wow, yeah, that's romantic and will totally win him over."

"And what do you know about winning over guys?"

His cheeks pinked, and he shrugged. "I'm just sayin', if you really like him, you need to be more sure of it."

I let him steer us away from whatever nerve I'd struck with my question. Toby knew he could talk to me whenever he needed. Maybe I'd revisit it, but he didn't seem to want to chat right then.

"So, did you and Mattie, you know, like *date* back in the day?" Toby asked.

I narrowed my eyes at him. "It's been *so* many years, I'm not sure I can recall that far back." He rolled his eyes, and I nudged him with my elbow. "No, we didn't date *back in the day*," I said. A flash of that kiss screamed through me, jolting me into awareness.

Toby studied me. "But you wanted to?"

I sighed again. "It's a long story. Suffice it to say that things were different back then."

"But you're glad he's back? Like you'd want to date him now?" Toby asked, a gleam of teasing mischief in his eyes.

Pointing a finger his way, I warned, "Don't even start. You can help us with ideas, but don't go mentioning anything to Mattie. He may be in a relationship already, and it's not my place to interfere."

"He's single," Toby quipped as he opened the fridge and grabbed an apple.

"Huh? What? How do you know that?"

He bit into the apple, juice spraying in tiny arcs, and chewed.

Loudly.

"I always wanted a horse when I was younger. Good to know my dreams came true with my dear nephew," I deadpanned.

Toby grinned broadly and took another bite.

"Oh my god," I griped. "Are you going to eat the whole thing before you answer my question?"

He smirked and finished chewing then opened his mouth to take another bite, but he paused. "I asked him." Toby took in the look on my face and rushed on. "Natalie's mom was at school the other day—probably just to flirt with the resource officer or something...seriously, Nat's so nice and her mom is the worst—anyway, I heard her telling the secretary about *fresh meat* who just moved into town." He shrugged. "Figured I'd warn him away from her."

"Toby, it's not really your place to police who Ms. Bell dates."

He scoffed. "She's a terrible person, and I like Mattie, I wasn't going to let him get caught in her web."

I couldn't help but laugh as he took another bite of

his apple. Patrice Bell truly was an awful person, and I had no idea how such a sweet kid like Natalie came from her. "So..." I hedged.

Toby smirked again. "He's single. Broke up with a boyfriend back in California and that's why he moved back home." He cocked his head. "Did you know he was gay?"

I nodded, lost in the memory of Mattie kissing me in the woods back before everything changed for us.

"Does he know you're gay?" my nephew pressed.

"No. At least, I don't think so. I didn't know—or hadn't admitted it—back then. He left and we didn't keep in touch."

Toby crossed his arms over his chest. "What happened between you two? Did you mess something up?"

"It's more complicated than that," I said. "It's not really something you need to know. We went our separate ways back then. We didn't fight or dislike each other, it's just the way things played out."

He studied me, looking so much like Tabby it was scary. "But you like him," he said. "You maybe didn't know back then, but you like him now."

"Don't you have homework or something to do?"

Toby grinned. "I'll go do my work, but I'm coming back because I have ideas."

"Oh lord, why does that sound so threatening?"

He waggled his brow. "Be prepared for greatness."

A knock sounded at the door.

"I'll just say hi to our new friend first," Toby said with a wicked grin.

"Behave," I warned.

He walked toward the door singing, "Sam and Mattie sitting in a tree, K-I-S-S-I-N-G."

"Tobias Benton," I said.

He laughed and opened the door. "Hi," he said, greeting Mattie brightly.

Mattie returned the greeting and walked through the door. "Wow, it's like looking in a mirror," he said as he took in our side of the duplex.

"Well, I'm going to go do homework while you two talk. About work. Work talk. For the job, of course." Toby gestured toward where I'd spread out on the kitchen table. "But don't get too far into it because I have ideas."

Mattie glanced between Toby and me, but eventually just clapped his hands together. "Sounds good, let's get down to business."

Toby headed toward his room while Mattie and I sat down at the kitchen table.

An hour later, we'd made a list of which artwork was going where around town, decided to just do the website from the bare bones, tagged which pieces were going to be on which pages of the site, and made a list of the locations around town we wanted to visit. We'd take notes and highlight those on the website.

"I think this is a great start," Mattie said.

Something must have shown on my face because he frowned. "You don't?"

"Just worried about the deadline. I've got other jobs looming, I need to do Christmas shopping, and adding this is just a lot." Toby and I had spent many Christmases as just the two of us, and I always worked hard to make sure he had a good holiday even when he was missing his mom. This year would be no different.

"I can help. Give me a shopping list, and I'll either search online or run over to White Pine and hit the mall," Mattie said, those big blue eyes as earnest and genuine as ever. "I'm not a web designer, but if there are any tasks a dummy can do, assign them to me. I can even do dinners some nights so you can keep working a little longer."

Something pulled in my heart. This was the Mattie I'd missed all those years. If I was being honest, this was the Mattie I'd fallen in love with back then and just not realized it until later. His eager generosity and authentic desire to help others were only two of the things I loved about this man.

But was it too late? Had I lost my chance way back then?

Toby said Mattie was single, but a little voice of doubt chittered insistently in my ear that he'd always be the one who got away.

As if the reminder of his single status needed a visual, Toby walked into the kitchen. I caught the quick waggle of his brow as he glanced between Mattie and me, but he covered it quickly and grabbed a cup from the cabinet.

Mattie and I watched with wide eyes and hidden smiles as Toby poured nearly a quart of milk into the cup and reached into the cookie package to retrieve not one, not two, not even three, but *five* chocolate chip cookies.

When he caught us watching, he popped a cookie into his mouth. "What?"

"We're having dinner," I said.

"In like an hour. I'm starving; don't worry, I'll eat." He sat down at the table and took a long swig of milk.

"The majority of my paychecks go to keeping him in milk," I pretended to whisper to Mattie.

"Whatever, I'm a growing boy. That's what your daddy group said."

Mattie chuckled and quirked a brow.

"They're not my *daddy group*," I said, but I couldn't help the smile. "I asked them about your leg pains. They asked if you were eating me out of house and home. When I told them yes, they said the leg pains were likely growing pains and eating like you'd been starved for days was normal."

Toby nodded. "See, it's fine. Now, do you want to hear my ideas?"

I gestured for him to go ahead.

"Okay, so Sugar Pines don't make the best Christmas trees. The other towns don't really have it that much better, but that's whatever." Toby popped another cookie in his mouth and swallowed it down with milk.

"So, I was thinking, instead of focusing on the pine tree part, we focus on the sugar part. So, how does sugar fit with Christmas?"

"Cookies? Candy? Desserts?" I offered.

"Yep, that's the way I was going too. So, I started with cookies. There are a ton of Christmas cookies, but one stands out." Toby paused as if waiting for us to figure it out.

"Sugar cookies?" Mattie hedged. "Snickerdoodles? Chocolate chip?"

"Think more along the lines of cookies you really only see around the holidays."

Finally, Mattie slapped the table. "Gingerbread cookies."

Toby beamed. "And that makes you think of..."

"Gingerbread houses," Mattie and I answered together.

The next thirty minutes were a cacophony of words and ideas being thrown around.

"Inaugural this year, and then annual."

"Make it a big competition. Gotta have great prizes."

"Bigger and better each year."

"Locals can enter at a discounted price."

"Different categories for kids and adults. Maybe this year, we just do traditional, but next year we can expand to categories like organic, homemade, building out of non-food items, life-sized, minis..."

The ideas grew and grew the longer the three of us talked.

When we finally called it quits, I knew we had something that would help Sugar Pine tremendously. And I was proud as hell of Toby.

Mattie gave him a fist pump before my nephew scurried to the basement to play video games with his friends online.

"Holy shit," Mattie said. "Not sure we would have come up with that on our own."

I shook my head. "I hadn't let my brain go in that direction."

"Kids are pretty amazing."

"I'm biased, but I definitely think this one is."

"You wanna get started on those tourist spots this week?" Mattie asked.

"Definitely." Our deadline was looming. I threw a glance over my shoulder at the kitchen calendar—we kept it color-coded so everyone knew about appointments, projects, etc. "Toby is spending this weekend at a friend's house. Let's do Saturday taking notes—that gives me time to gut the website and get the basics built back up before we start putting things in. And if either of us is out and about, we should talk things up with the businesses around town. See what we can get them to commit to as far as really helping to sell the holidays in Sugar Pine."

"Perfect," Mattie said as he stood and headed toward the door. "I'm going to be working on a few pieces the next couple days." His words held a bit of a warning.

"So, we should check in on you and make sure you're hydrated and fed?"

"You remember." A soft smile played on his lips.

My insides warmed at all I remembered about Mattie, but I just nodded. "We'll make sure you don't perish mid-project."

FIVE

*Mattie*

THE KNOCK at my door came as I wandered into the kitchen for a drink.

I'd been busy the last few days working on commissioned pieces, finalizing some pieces to hang around town, and chatting up some of the business owners regarding ways they could get involved in making Sugar Pine a top holiday destination in Evergreen County, the state, and beyond.

When I poured myself into my work, I lost hours at a time painting, editing photos, or framing pieces.

But I'd set a timer to remind myself to eat, drink, and take bathroom breaks.

Pulling open the door, I found Toby.

"Sam sent me over to make sure you weren't dead," the kid said. "He's working on the website, but he told me to tell you about the stickers."

I smiled and stepped back so he could enter. I didn't

know if it was because Toby reminded me of myself at that age, he resembled Sam in a way, or just because he was such a good kid, but I enjoyed the times he'd pop in to help or just to look at my work.

"I was just getting ready to stuff my face with cookies, you want some?"

He shrugged in the nonchalant way of teens, but I could almost see his mouth watering. "Sure."

"Milk?"

"Yeah. Please," he tacked on as if remembering Sam would have something to say about his lack of manners.

I poured two glasses of milk, giving him the larger one after seeing the way the kid could put away milk and cookies, and motioned toward the table.

Once he'd demolished two Oreos and several gulps of milk, I asked, "So, what's this about stickers?"

Toby brightened. "My friend Jasper," he started, and I didn't miss the way his cheeks pinked a bit. "Their dad has this printing business. Mostly sells stuff online, but he said he'd be glad to help out with stickers and stuff for Sugar Pine. He just needs a logo or image or whatever, and the wording."

"That's awesome," I said, already thinking about the logo. "Your..." I paused and cocked my head. "Sorry, do you call Sam your dad? Your uncle?"

Toby shrugged. "Mostly just Sam, but uncle works. He and Mom always just said uncle or Sam or Uncle Sam, so *Dad* never really fit."

"Makes sense," I said. "Sam and I can work on the logo and some images for the stickers."

Toby ate another cookie. "When I was younger," he started, and I had to remind myself not to laugh at a fourteen-year-old referring to his younger days. "I used to want to call him Dad since my friends had dads."

His words hit me right in the heart. "Damn, I get that. My dad traveled a lot for business and was almost never home." I'd later figure out he was also having affairs all over the globe, but the kid didn't need to hear that. "All I ever wanted was to look out into the sea of parents and see my dad. But I think he made one baseball game. Never did come to any of my theater performances— don't really think he tried too hard since he didn't think theater was worthwhile."

"I get that," Toby said, his eyes bright and earnest. "Sam is at every single thing I do, but it sucks to know Mom has to miss over half my life. And my real dad is probably out there somewhere playing catch with his other kids, watching their games, going to their open houses at school."

Shit. The kid was killing me.

"I mean," he went on, "I know Mom has a really important job, and she makes it up to me when she's home. And Sam's the best. Just sucks to think about my real dad out there with his *real* family."

"Would you ever want to meet him?" I asked.

"Sometimes I think I would, but most of the time I'm just mad that he knew Mom was pregnant, and he just left her." He nibbled at a cookie. "There's this kid in my homeroom—we've been in school together forever—and he's adopted, but he knows his bio mom. She got pregnant really young and gave him up for adoption. But now she's married and has other kids. He mostly says it's cool, but makes me wonder if he ever feels like me and hates the fact she's got whole other family." After draining his milk, he shrugged. "But I know I'm lucky to have Sam and Mom. Just wish she was home more."

"Once she's back, she'll be here for almost a year?"

He nodded. "Yeah, it's nice when she's home, just sucks when she's gone. But I still get to talk to her."

"What does Sam do when she's home?"

Toby cocked his head. "Mostly the same stuff as now, but he kinda lets her take over. He goes places more, takes little trips if he has time." He shot a glance my way. "Goes on dates."

"Oh yeah?" I forced the grin. "I bet he's got the ladies lined up waiting for your mom to get home." The words were meant to be light, but they fell like a brick.

Toby smirked. "The only time any lady tried to date him got really awkward when he told her he was gay, and then she made it even worse when she pretended like she knew that and was just trying to set him up with her brother. At least, that's the story my mom teases him about."

My kitchen ran out of oxygen.

Sam was gay.

I mean, I'd gotten vibes back then.

Or maybe I should say I'd hoped against hope back then.

But there it was.

Spelled out plain and simple.

Toby bit his lip and pushed back from the table. "Well, I have homework. Gotta go. Don't forget the stickers."

The front door slammed shut.

Several minutes later, I blinked myself back to awareness.

Well, fuck.

I definitely wasn't getting any more work done for the day.

## SIX
## Sam

RUBBING my tired eyes and trying to convince myself the dull ache in my hands wasn't arthritis, I stretched and stood from my computer. We were much too close to the deadline for me to feel comfortable, but the website was at least to the point of being ready for us to add in artwork and local features.

Mattie and I had chatted over text and confirmed we'd both been spreading the word around Sugar Pine as well as gathering information. We'd agreed to go scout out a few places together, but the main work was soon going to be putting all the information into catchy, easy-to-understand text so visitors to the website found themselves curious about Sugar Pine.

"Can I eat dinner over at Jasper's?" Toby asked, his backpack already on his shoulder. He and Jasper had been friends since Kindergarten, but they'd been spending a lot more time together recently. They had a large group of friends, but the two of them were joined at the hip.

"Did Jasper's mom say it's okay?" I asked, glancing at the clock and realizing I'd need to fix dinner soon. My stomach growled. I could eat and relax for the evening. Or I could eat and get back to work on the website.

"Yeah, she's fixing lasagna. The good kind."

I snorted. "It's a frozen lasagna from the store. I make it from scratch. Once, I even made the noodles with my own two hands and you'd still rather have a frozen store brand. Where did I go wrong?"

Toby grinned. "Save yourself some time. The frozen kind just tastes better."

"Blasphemy." I tapped my wrist. "Home by nine. It's a school night. Be polite and don't do anything stupid."

"Yeah, yeah, I know," Toby said. "Have fun tonight."

"I will. Love you." Then his words registered. "Wait, what?"

But he was already out the door.

Frowning, I opened a cupboard and let it slam shut.

Next, the fridge.

Nothing.

Freezer.

Nada.

I needed to eat, but nothing sounded good.

I could go to the diner, but I didn't really want to leave the house.

As I was contemplating a peanut butter and jelly

sandwich or a plate of bagel bites, a knock sounded at the door.

Pulling open the door, a rush of cold bulldozing into the front room made me wonder if Toby had put on a heavy enough coat—and knowing in the deepest regions of my soul he likely had on shorts and a hoodie, and I was the worst parent in the world for letting him out of the house like that...but honestly, have you ever tried to talk sense into a teenager? The. Worst.

Anyway, Mattie sidled his way into the house with a warm smile.

And a bag of food looking suspiciously like it came from the diner.

"Toby said you needed help with something." He shrugged. "Then he shoved this bag in my hands, told me he'd ordered it by mistake and not to let it go to waste, and that he'd be gone until nine."

I blinked.

And blinked again.

Then I chuckled and pinched the bridge of my nose. "He's just like his mom."

Mattie cocked his head. "Huh?"

"Never mind."

Mattie shook the bag. "Are you busy? Want to take a break for dinner?"

Trying to decide if I should throttle my nephew or thank him profusely, I gestured toward the table. "I'll grab plates."

Ten minutes later, with a spread of diner food before

us, we were chatting and laughing just like old times. Things had always been so easy with Mattie and me, and I was grateful that hadn't changed.

"What made you want to come back to Sugar Pine?" I asked, munching on a fry.

"I think I knew pretty quickly into my journey to California that I wasn't meant to be out there, at least not forever. I liked it; it was gorgeous, but I never felt at home." The look on his face told me he was far away. "The first few years were just me trying to get my feet under me; never had the phrase *starving artist* been so spot on. Then I finally got a client base, settled in, started making good money, and spent most of my time trying to convince myself that artists had to suffer and being sad and lonely out there was good for my art."

My frown was automatic.

He shrugged. "It wasn't all bad. I made a few moves, learned a lot about myself, and met some great people. A few years ago, I met this guy. We hit it off pretty quickly and got serious. Longest relationship I've ever been in."

"But?" I wanted to hear it from Mattie and not just Toby.

"Things got messy. He wanted to open the relationship up after a year or so, and I wasn't willing. Don't get me wrong, I don't fault polyamory or open relationships, it's just not for me. He was angry and said I was stubborn and didn't care about his feelings. I was hurt and felt like he wanted a lot more than I could offer. In the end, I figured out he'd been cheating even before he suggested we open things up, and it got worse after. The breakup hurt, but it was for the best." Mattie took a long swallow of his water. "I wallowed for a few weeks, but then I woke up one morning and knew what I needed to do. It sounds cliché, but the saying *home is where your heart is* kept floating through my head and I couldn't get back here fast enough."

"Do you regret leaving?"

Mattie nodded. "Sometimes, yeah. I regret leaving the way I did. I fucked things up and then ran off. I should have stayed to make sure everything was okay. Other times, I'm glad I had the experience out there because it helped make me who I am today—improved my art big time."

"I'm sorry about the breakup," I offered.

"It happened on Christmas which really sucked. I think that's why I'm looking forward to Christmas here this year. Need some happy memories." His eyes met mine. "I really am sorry for the way things went down back then."

I shook my head. "No reason to be."

"Toby told me a story yesterday," Mattie hedged.

"Oh lord," I groaned. "What?"

"About some lady asking you out on a date, but then things got awkward when you told her you're gay." He stopped. Mattie's eyes bore into mine as if daring me to deny it in the heavy silence.

"It was even worse when she tried to convince me

she'd just been trying to set me up with her brother," I said with a chuckle.

"When did you know?" Mattie asked, friendly and easygoing as usual, but his words slightly tinged by hurt.

I shook my head, remembering how overwhelming everything had been back then. "I think there'd been hints for a few months, but I wasn't picking up on them, or I wasn't allowing myself to acknowledge them. Then Tabby got pregnant, and you left. Part of me wanted so badly to follow you."

"Instead, I freaked you out by kissing you. Then like some damn kid in a teen drama, I walked away thinking if you really liked me, you'd chase after me. But you let me leave so I spent the next decade thinking I'd messed everything up." Mattie's eyes gleamed. "I shouldn't have put you in that position."

"You didn't know everything going on with Tabby at that point. It wasn't like you purposely put me in any kind of position."

"Sometimes I wonder what would have happened if I'd stayed." Mattie balled up his sandwich wrapper.

"No reason to think about that," I said. "You needed to leave, I had to stay. Things were the way they were." I cleared my throat and caught his eyes. "Doesn't mean things are the same now."

## SEVEN

# Mattie

"THAT SOUNDS ABSOLUTELY PERFECT," Sam said as we wrapped up our meeting with Delores at the Sugar Pine bakery.

She'd gotten wind of our work to bring in more visitors in the winter and had a laundry list of things she wanted to do at the bakery. Delores had even gotten the coffee shop next door to commit to special winter flavors for their coffees and teas.

Sugar Pine Baked Goods would carry a line of sugar plum items including sugar plum tarts, sugar plum crumble, and sugar plum coffee cake along with an assortment of gingerbread sweets. One Lump or Two would offer a sugar plum coffee and tea, a gingerbread chai latte, and a gingerbread dark roast.

"We're looking forward to putting Sugar Pine back in competition with the rest of the county," Delores said.

"And you better believe I'll be entering my very own gingerbread house in the competition."

We waved and the little jingle bells chimed above us as we walked out into the bright but cold December day.

"Even if we don't get the grant, I think the whole town is excited to bring Sugar Pine back to its prime," I said, zipping my coat against the frigid air.

"We're getting that grant," Sam said. "Or at least we're going to have our proposal submitted for it. I'm not losing out on the money; the town needs it too badly."

I bumped into him. "You were always so competitive."

He shrugged.

"Last stop," I said as we neared the edge of the woods. Sugar Pine was covered with deciduous and evergreen forests, but this particular wooded area was where the town had gotten its not-quite-accurate name.

It was a gorgeous location with great hiking trails, perfect spots overlooking the Pine River, and small areas for camping while watching the stars.

It was also where I kissed Sam fourteen years ago.

But I wasn't thinking about that.

Much.

We followed the easiest trail into the heart of the woods. "I think we focus on the trails, the great view of the river, and how clear and bright the stars are on a crisp winter night," I said.

"Do we combine this part with the cabins and the lodge? Or keep them separate?" Sam asked.

"Separate. There will be folks who want the comfort of the cabins and the convenience of the lodge, while others will want the more rustic experience. We're not going to convince the types who want to stay at the White Pine Hotel, so we need to hook the more outdoorsy crew."

"And get the ones who want the small-town hotel experience to at least come to Sugar Pine to check out the shops, take pictures for social media by the river, and ohhh and ahhh over the gingerbread houses," Sam said. He tapped notes on his phone about what we wanted to say about Pine River, the trails, the camping, and the view. "Oh, almost forgot, I sent the logo and images to Jasper's dad for the stickers."

"Perfect. I dropped the artwork off at the lodge. They were excited to get the pieces hung above the fireplace and in the cabins." Not gonna lie, a streak of pride coursed through me at knowing my work would be seen by locals and visitors alike.

Sam stopped and I nearly slammed into him. He glanced around the cold, dim woods, dappled December sunlight decorating the ground. Then he turned, his deep brown eyes meeting mine as our breaths mingled in icy puffs.

"Do you remember that day?" His words were low, punctuated by the soft, cold breeze and birds singing their early-winter songs.

I'd known we were at *that* tree before he even spoke.

As if I could ever forget that day.

We'd gone on a hike and gotten tickled about something. When we'd stopped at the tree, everything played out like our own little telenovela.

Sam, leaning against a tree.

Me, stepping closer.

Our breaths mingling with the scent of pine and fallen leaves as the autumn wind suggested only a short time until she threw in the towel.

And I'd brushed my lips over his.

When I pulled back, there'd been confusion and curiosity in his eyes.

I'd pressed our mouths together again.

Sam hadn't pushed me away, but he'd whispered, "Mattie, I can't."

Embarrassment and hurt warred in my heart, the need to run away mixing with the desire to make him realize how good we'd be together.

In the end, there'd been no convincing.

No explanations.

I'd turned to leave, so sure he'd chase after me and make things right.

Instead, he'd let me go.

"Yeah," I croaked.

"What do you think would have happened if I'd kissed you back?" he asked, his words soft with courageous fear.

Chuckling, I stared at his lips. "Knowing my horny

ass, I would have dropped to my knees and sucked you off."

"Shit, Mattie," Sam choked out.

"You asking for a reason?" A woodpecker tapped out a rapid rhythm in the distance, the sound echoing the beat of my heart.

"What if you kissed me again, and I didn't pull back?" Sam's words whooshed from him on a whispered breath.

"Knowing my horny ass," I started with a grin, "I'd drop to my knees and suck you off."

Sam chuckled, but fire blazed in the brown depths of his eyes.

"Do you want me to kiss you?" Fourteen years of worrying I'd fucked things up between us tumbled away, replaced by all the heavy want and wishful longing I'd kept buried away.

He snaked an arm around my waist and pulled me close. "I've wanted you to kiss me since the day you came home." And then our lips connected, heat exploding between us.

The disappointment of all those years ago melted away as Sam's tongue met mine, his mouth hot and demanding. Hands roamed, delving beyond coat zippers to seek the warm, solid planes of chests and shoulders. Fingers trailing over soft curves, our hips pressed together in a desperate quest for friction.

Sam's hungry mouth devoured mine while his fingers fought a frantic battle with the button and zipper on my jeans. When I unzipped my coat and yanked up my shirt, Sam smirked and pressed another kiss to my lips before dropping to his knees.

"Wanna do this and more when we have more time," he mumbled, brushing his nose against my belly button.

"And a heater," I added before biting my lip.

This was happening.

He hadn't pulled away.

Sam Benton kissed me back.

And he didn't let me go.

He nuzzled my cock and brought his big, brown eyes up to meet mine.

I nodded.

"Tell me," he demanded.

"Suck me."

Sam pushed my boxers down and tucked them under my balls. The cold air teased, but his hot, wet mouth took me in, saving me from the frigid breeze.

"Holy shit," I mumbled, reaching over him to hold myself up with hands pressed into the tree trunk. "Fuck, Sam. So good."

The kiss had been magical.

The blowjob was a dream come true.

Clearly, Sam had a way with his mouth.

He fisted my length and sucked me until my knees nearly buckled. The soft cup of my balls while he gazed up at me with something so much deeper than friendship sent me over the edge.

"Fuck," I cried out. "Gonna come."

Sam swallowed every drop I pumped into his greedy mouth, and when I yanked him up to kiss me, he groaned against my lips, sharing the flavor of my load with me.

Shoving him against the tree, I nodded toward his jacket.

"Unzip it."

Eyes on mine, he followed directions.

"Now your jeans."

Done.

"Pull out your cock."

Sam lazily shoved his underwear down and took himself in hand as he smirked, his eyes never leaving mine. "Your turn," he challenged.

Dropping to my knees, I pressed a kiss to his naval, swirling my tongue around the protruding belly button. Working my way lower, I buried my nose in his pubes and breathed him in deeply, his scent burned into me for eternity.

Sam lifted his arms and sought purchase in the bark, but the moment I took him between my lips, his hands flew to my head, fingers twisting in the jaw-length locks. "Fuck, Mattie."

He tasted every bit as delicious as I'd always known he would.

Yet, I wasn't sad we'd missed out on this all those years ago.

Having Sam here and now was meant to be.

We were the men we'd been born to be.

No secrets.

No wondering if there was something better out there for us.

Just two men whose friendship had withstood the long years and eventually traveled full circle.

"Fuck. Fuck. Fuck, Mattie," Sam chanted. "Oh shit, gonna come."

His hot load exploded on my tongue, and I breathed hard and fast through my nose as I swallowed what he gave me. With a final thrust of his hips, Sam gave a gentle tug on my hair and pulled me to stand.

We kissed for several long, slow moments until an icy gust of wind reminded us to get our asses back home.

"Toby is staying at Jasper's tonight," Sam said.

"My place?"

He nodded.

We all but ran home.

By the time we reached the duplex, our synapses were firing normally again. I still had every intention of getting him into my bed, but we'd emerged from the post-nut haze enough to act mostly like adults.

"I'm going to check in on Toby and order some food for later," Sam said as he hefted off his backpack. "What time you want me to come over?"

"Um." I ran a hand through my hair. "Thought I'd jump in the shower first."

"Yeah, same."

"An hour or so?" I moved closer and leaned in to nuzzle his jawline. "Make the food something that can keep or schedule the delivery for later." I nibbled his neck. "*Much* later."

Sam gripped the back of my neck and devoured my mouth. "Sounds like a plan."

Just over an hour later, I'd prepped, showered, and put some wine in the fridge. Glancing around my bedroom, I did a quick mental checklist. Changed the sheets. Waters on the bedside table. Lube. Condoms available. Lights dimmed, candles burning, and curtains drawn.

Perfect.

A knock sounded at the door, and I went to let Sam in.

The way his eyes traveled up my flannel pants to my bare chest sent a thrill coursing through me. He walked through the door, brushed a kiss to my cheek, and slipped off his slides before holding up a deli bag. "Figured subs would wait for us."

I grabbed the bag, unloaded the subs and pasta salad into the fridge, and put the chips on the counter. "Toby good?"

Sam's eyes softened and he smiled. "Yeah, the little matchmaker is fine. He'll be at Jasper's all weekend."

Wrapping my arms around his waist and pushing him into the corner of the counter, I grinned. "So, we have the whole weekend to get as dirty as we want?"

Sam rolled his hips, his hard cock rubbing against mine through his lounge pants. "All weekend."

Something telling crossed his face and I kissed him. "No worries, we'll work on the site during downtime."

He chuckled and pressed his forehead to mine. "Oh, thank god. I wanna be here with you, but the deadline is killing me."

"We'll get it done." I nuzzled my nose against his.

The heat simmering between us blazed to life when Sam gripped my chin and owned my mouth. Yanking on his shirt, I pulled him to my bedroom and locked the door behind us.

He stripped out of his clothes and stroked himself, watching me.

"Fuck," I muttered, shucking my pants to the floor, stepping close, and walking him backward to the bed. "Top or bottom?"

"I like to flip, but I can go either way if you only do one or the other."

"Fuck," I said again, capturing his mouth for a wet, sloppy kiss. "Love to flip."

"I brought condoms if we..." he started.

"I have some too."

"I haven't been with anyone since my last physical and negative test." His fiery eyes caught mine as his words sank in.

Oh shit.

I'd never ditched the condoms with anyone.

Hadn't ever truly trusted anyone enough to think about it.

But with Sam, I had no doubts.

"My tests were negative," I answered.

"Without?"

I nodded, breathless emotion clogging my throat too much to speak.

"Get on the bed," Sam ordered.

Scrambling to comply, I spread out on the king-sized mattress and reached for him. He grabbed the lube and tossed it on the bed before cuddling close and taking my dick to the back of his throat.

I groaned and thrust my hips, loving his hot tongue swirling over my shaft. When he licked his fingers and worked them between my ass cheeks, I whimpered, "Please, Sam."

"Hand me the lube."

Nearly throwing it at him, I gripped the base of my cock as he coated his fingers. When he tongued my slit and worked his lubed fingers into my crack, I cried out. Sam opened me slowly and gently, sucking me softly as his fingers breached my hole and stretched my tight ring.

"Oh god, Sam, please."

"What do you want?"

"Give me that dick," I begged.

Sam moved between my legs and shoved a pillow under my ass. Lining his cockhead up with my hole, he pressed in slowly. Inch by inch, he owned my body. My breath caught at the slick, bare heat of his cock buried in my ass.

"God, Mattie, look how you open for me." He stroked my cock. "You look so pretty on my cock."

He dropped to his elbows and took my mouth, our tongues mating in a hot, desperate dance as he thrust into me over and over.

"Never been with someone like this," he whispered against my mouth. "Never been bare with anyone else. Only you, Mattie."

My heart soared, and I knew everything from our pasts had led us right to this moment in time. He was my person, my future, my everything. He'd been that back then, but it hadn't been right. This year when I celebrated Christmas, I'd do it with the love of my life by my side.

"Fuck, Sam. So good. Oh god, I'm close."

He stilled. "Wanna feel you inside me when you come."

The growl escaping my chest filled the room. "Move to the edge of the bed."

Sam pulled out gently and positioned himself on his back with his ass on the edge. Kissing the inside of his knees, I moved his legs to rest over my shoulders before I grabbed the lube and slicked my cock.

With the excess liquid, I teased his pucker and worked him open. "Gonna fill this pretty hole with my cum."

Sam's glistening cock jerked against his stomach.

The exquisite heat of his body gripped me tightly as I inched into him. He hissed as his body stretched around me and fisted his cock.

"Jack yourself off, wanna see you come before I give you my load."

Sam stroked himself as I pumped my hips, my slick cock sliding in and out as my balls pressed against the fleshy globes of his ass.

My orgasm was too close, but we had all the time in the world. As badly as I wanted to savor the moment, my balls screamed for release. "Fuck, Sam. I'm close. Come for me."

He worked his fist up and down his dick before grunting and shooting creamy white stripes onto his chest and belly.

With his hole clenching around me, I gave in to my release and poured every bit of myself into his body. My cock pulsed shot after shot deep in his ass, and I buried my face in his calf with a groan as he milked every drop from me.

When we finally caught our breaths and cuddled together on the first spare inch of the bed we came to in our hurry to hold each other, I cupped Sam's face and kissed him. "That was definitely worth the wait."

He grinned and nodded with a grunt.

Eventually, we maneuvered ourselves to the head of the mattress but stayed curled together. When both our stomachs growled, we chuckled and rolled from bed. After soaping up and rinsing off quickly in the shower, we made our way to the kitchen to gather a picnic of sorts.

Back in bed, Sam checked in with Toby.

The kid sent a gif of a little boy singing the *sitting in a tree K-I-S-S-I-N-G* song.

"Little shit." Sam laughed and tossed his phone.

"He's lucky to have you," I said. "I know he misses his mom, and he's got a lot of feelings about his bio dad, but he appreciates you being here."

"This parenting gig is the hardest thing I've ever done," Sam said as he opened his sandwich. "But I can't imagine not being here for him."

"Like I said, he's lucky." I spooned up some pasta salad. "My dad was never around. I used to blame his job, but I learned as I got older it was more the affairs and him just choosing not to be there. He wasn't good for Mom, so in the end, it was for the best, I guess. I always swore if I got into a relationship or became a parent, I'd do everything in my power to *be there*."

"When Tabby got pregnant and said she wanted to keep the baby, I was terrified. It wasn't like I *wanted* her to have an abortion, it was her body and her decision completely, and I swore I'd support her whatever she decided. But all I could think of was how shitty our parents had been and what if that was all we knew. Was the baby doomed before he was even born?"

I gripped the back of his neck and pulled him in for a long, slow kiss. "Looks like you two did a great job. Toby is a good kid."

Sam pulled back, a dazed look in his eyes. "Why is this so easy with you?"

I smiled. "When it's right, it's right."

"Even back then," he hedged.

Nodding, I took another bite of pasta salad. "Even back then, we were right, our timing was just off."

"What if sex makes things awkward between us?" Sam asked.

I shook my head. "Nope. We won't let it. We're not some young, dumb kids anymore. We're adults. We've always been good together. Even better now that we know ourselves more."

## EIGHT

## Sam

CHECKING to make sure Toby was in the basement playing his video games, I clapped my hands together. "Okay, let's see what you got."

Mattie grinned and placed four large bags on the table. "This was fun. I haven't shopped for a kid in...well, I guess forever."

"Whoa, this looks like more than I put on the list." I peered into the bags. "I gave you a price limit." Money wasn't a *huge* issue, but I wasn't made of millions. Plus, I didn't want Toby thinking he'd always get *everything* on his wish list.

Mattie shrugged and held his thumb and finger apart about half an inch. "I only went over a bit." He wrinkled his nose and blushed. "And anything over can be considered from me."

I rolled my eyes, but sighed and pulled him close. "I thought the gift from us together was going to be his sleepover. You can't back out now, I need you here if I'm going to survive four teen boys hopped up on sugar and adrenaline."

"I've gotchu," Mattie said with a grin. "Let's look through these before he comes upstairs. I want to get things returned if they're wrong."

Laughing, I shook my head. "He won't emerge from his man cave until he smells food."

"Gee, I wonder where he learned to pour himself into his work and not take a break for hours?" Mattie teased. I gave him a pointed look and he flushed. "Oh, right. I'll keep my mouth shut."

"Mmhm, that's what I thought."

The gifts Mattie bought were perfect, and I thanked him profusely with a long, slow kiss.

"Mmm, maybe I should go shopping for you more often," Mattie said, his arms wrapping me in a hug as he pressed our bodies together.

"You saved my ass," I said. "Thank you."

"I happen to be very fond of your ass, so I had ulterior motives."

After dinner, Toby helped with the dishes before retreating to his room for a video chat with Tabby and finishing homework.

While I packed Toby's lunches for the week, Mattie scrolled through the single dads' forum on my laptop.

"Ohh, this one should be good," he said. "One of the mods made a pinned post. 'What's the hardest part of parenting so far? If you're comfortable, share your child/children's ages with your answers.'" He read quietly for a moment then started sharing some of them with me.

*Dad I am*: *My son is 14 and I'd like to think we've gotten over the hard parts. I was only 17 when my girlfriend at the time told me the news. I wasn't prepared to be a dad, but we did the best we could. Even got married and tried to make it work for a few years, but that fizzled out. We finally divorced three years ago after being separated for a bit. Now I'm juggling being a single dad and trying not to burn out from work.*

*DiamondDaddy*: *I envy those of you already into teenage years with your children. My son was just born, and I am already finding that the hardest part is balance. How do I, someone who had always planned to stay a confirmed bachelor and who is a self-proclaimed workaholic, balance my time without losing, well... ME in the process? I had an absent father, and I don't want to be that for my son. I want to be THERE. But staying true to myself and being a present parent is more difficult than I anticipated. There never seems to be enough hours in the day.*

Some of the answers took me back to Toby as an infant. A few of the answers sent dread coursing through me.

"What would your answer be? I can type it for you."

I thought for a moment before saying, "I'd likely say something like, 'My nephew is 14. (His mom is my twin sister, and she's deployed for 6-12 months at a time. When she's gone, I'm a dad and uncle all rolled into one.) So far, the hardest has just been doing it all alone when his mom is gone. I know I'm lucky that she's home for long stretches of time too, and not everyone has that break. I never planned to be a parent, and this shit is scary. Looking back, I think the times he was sick were probably when I felt the most helpless. Watching him go off to school was the very definition of bittersweet. Not sure how I'm going to handle him getting his license in the next couple years. Excuse me while I go bury my head in the sand for a bit.'"

Mattie typed as I spoke, but when he reached the end, he looked at me with wide eyes. "Oh my god, I hadn't even thought about watching him drive off in a car. And moving away for college? Shit."

"Okay, enough depressing shit," I said with a chuckle. "Let's just enjoy the time we've got." While I loved the thought of Mattie and I watching Toby progress through his teen years together, I didn't have the heart to think about my kid being grown and on his own.

At least not right then.

"I don't know why Darcy thinks we both need to show this guy around," I grumbled. "We still have a deadline looming."

"Christmas is in a week," Mattie said.

As if that fact would console me.

"Which means the deadline is *less* than a week."

"Darcy said this guy is doing stories on all four Evergreen County towns. He thinks we'd be best to show him around as a team."

It made sense. Mattie and I had been the ones gathering all the info for the new website. We'd been the ones to come up with the gingerbread house contest—thanks to Toby. Aside from Darcy, we were probably the best to show this reporter around and try to sell Sugar Pine to his audience.

But a mayor I was not, and all I could think about was the deadline. I worked well with a deadline usually. This one was just way too close. Sighing, I said, "Fine, but we're giving him quick and easy."

Mattie wagged his brow. "Sounds fun."

When we met up with Rafe, my heart sank. He was absolutely gorgeous.

Great body, great smile, charismatic.

And he definitely had eyes for Mattie.

But Rafe kept things professional throughout our little tour of Sugar Pine, asking questions, making comments, taking notes.

At our last stop near the mayor's office, I paused to

check a text from Toby. When I caught up with Mattie and Rafe, I heard the reporter ask Mattie out for drinks.

With my heart in my throat, I prepared to hear the worst.

"There's one of my favorite people," Darcy crowed, ripping me away from my eavesdropping. "How'd the tour go? Did you wrap him around your little pinky and promise him whatever he wanted if he made Sugar Pine out to be the best town in Evergreen County?" The little man beamed, his eyes bright with mischief.

*Pretty sure Mattie is promising him whatever he wants right now.* The thought stabbed at my heart, but I cleared my throat and offered what I hoped was a convincing smile. "He seemed to like what he saw."

"Good, good," Darcy said, rubbing his hands together. "I knew you boys were the perfect team to show him around. Now we just need to meet that deadline and get that grant." He elbowed me good-naturedly.

As if I needed a reminder of the deadline.

The thought of working on the website over the next few days while imagining Mattie with Rafe had me ready to toss my Christmas cookies.

## NINE

## Mattie

"YOU HAVE *GOT* to be kidding me," Sam growled from his office.

High winds had been blowing through Sugar Pine all day wreaking havoc on the power, the internet, and anything not tied down.

Sam had taken to working furiously during the periods of functioning power and internet, however those two things hadn't been cooperating over the last hour or so.

He stomped into the kitchen where I'd lit a couple candles to ward off the darkness as the afternoon winter sun sank lower on the horizon, and the winds continued to batter our little town.

"Is that coffee?" His words were a grumbled plea.

I grabbed two mugs and filled them with coffee. "It is. I'm going to heat up some soup. Figure I'll pop some bread in the oven and keep my fingers crossed the power

73

holds at least until the bread is crusty and warm. Hoping the power doesn't go out completely, but having the oven on for a while will at least help keep the kitchen warm for a bit if it does."

Sam sighed. "I really can't afford to keep losing time on this project. I know Sugar Pine needs the grant, and I want us to get it, but at this point it's turned into a personal challenge just to make sure I don't fail at getting this submitted in time." He sipped his coffee. "Mmmm, that's good. Thank you." Sam leaned in to kiss my cheek, but a shadow of something played around his eyes.

He'd been a bit strange since the day we took Rafe around town.

*Off* was probably the best word for it.

I'd chalked it up to the stress of the deadline, but something niggled at the back of my mind. Did Sam regret that we'd started something? Was having me here cramping his style?

The power flickered off.

Sam cursed.

I didn't regret the two of us working on the grant project. It had given us the push we needed to explore things between us. But I did feel bad that Sam got stuck with the more stressful part of the job.

I took him in my arms and buried my face in his neck. "I know you need to work, I just wanted to let you know—"

He tensed in my arms. "I know—" he interrupted.

"You know what?"

"You've met someone," Sam said, his words laced with stress and defeat.

Pulling back, I frowned and searched his face. "Huh?"

Sam extricated himself from my arms and ran his hands through his hair. "I've been waiting for this, just wasn't sure when you'd tell me. I heard Rafe ask you out." He huffed out a laugh and held his hands up. "And I get it, I totally do. He's gorgeous. He probably goes all over to get the scoop on fascinating stories. We haven't made any commitments, so it's an easy break—"

"Sam—"

"And we can just go back to—"

"Sam." The tone of my voice caught him that time.

"Huh?"

"Shut. Up." The tightness in my chest was a combination of emotions, but I breathed as evenly as possible as I crowded Sam against the kitchen counter. "Just shut up," I said, softer this time, cupping his face in my hands. "Do you really think I'd be having sex with you and looking to go out with someone else?"

I didn't give Sam time to answer.

"And yes, Rafe was gorgeous. Yes, he asked me out. Did you happen to hear me tell him I was involved with someone?" I nuzzled my nose against his. "I don't care if he travels the world, I've got all I need right here."

"But—"

"No buts..." I paused. "Unless you're not on the same page about us?"

"I am, I just thought—"

"No, that's just it," I said, brushing a kiss over his lips. "You *didn't* think. I'm going to blame the stress of the holidays and the deadline for making you dumb." I kissed the corner of his mouth where his lips quirked into a tiny smile. "I'm not going out with Rafe. I have a hot single dad and his son to spend time with this holiday."

"This holiday?" Sam whispered.

I grinned. "And beyond."

Sam pressed his forehead to mine. "Mattie?"

"Huh?"

"I love you," he whispered.

My entire body froze.

"Sorry, that's probably too soon and too much—"

"Shut. Up." Blinking through stinging eyes, I swallowed thickly. "I love you too."

Wrapping him in my arms, I brought our lips together and let the kiss carry us away until Toby came pounding up the stairs grumbling about being hungry.

Ice pelted the windows a few days before Christmas, and I breathed a sigh of relief that Toby was at Jasper's house, so he didn't have to witness Sam's mental breakdown.

"No, no, no." Sam's words barely drowned out the meteorologist's forecast on the television.

The weather forecast called for enough ice to shut everything down—and for those in the Midwest, it was common knowledge that the slightest bit of ice coating the entire town could do that.

"But the good news is," the meteorologist yammered on, "in true Midwest weather fashion, tomorrow looks to be jingling in with above-average temperatures so the ice will melt quickly, and we'll be looking at perfect Christmas weather." She beamed, white teeth glowing on the screen, and went on to talk about the chances of a white Christmas being very low this year.

"You've probably got a while before the ice causes problems," I said, pressing a kiss to Sam's head as he sat hunched over his desk. "Give me things to do if it helps, and work until you can't. Maybe we'll luck out and not even lose power."

Sam huffed. "Did your time in California make you forget everything about winters here?"

"Where's your Christmas spirit?" I teased and let him pull me onto his lap. "Let's think positively. Maybe we can manifest internet and power that works throughout the ice storm."

Sam chuckled and buried his face in my neck. "Pretty sure my manifestation skills are lacking. They definitely didn't help me during nights of teething and ear infections."

We made out for a long moment until a cheery little jingle sounded from the TV where Mayor Joseph preened and invited people to participate in Sugar Pine's inaugural Gingerbread House Extravaganza.

Sam slapped my ass. "That's a sign from the universe

that I need to get back to work. I need you to get on the website and look for anything that doesn't work. Links, tabs, images not loading, that kind of thing. Make specific note of what's not working and any errors you get."

Relieved to have something to do rather than sit around like a bum while Sam worked, I set to work as the ice continued to come down.

We fell into a productive rhythm spurred on by the looming deadline and when the internet went out about three hours later, I had a detailed list of errors. Luckily, there weren't many, and Sam didn't seem *too* stressed over what he needed to check on.

He ran a hand over his face. "I'll be glad when the town can get an internet upgrade."

"You needed a break anyway. Let's shower and throw those pizzas in the oven before the power goes out."

Two hours later, we'd both showered and stuffed ourselves on pizza when the power flickered out. I cleaned up the kitchen in candlelight while Sam made notes on my list as he paced the kitchen.

"Did you talk to Toby?" I asked.

"Yeah, he's good. They're all snug and cozy at Jasper's. I told him he needed to stay put until the ice melted tomorrow at least."

I caught Sam around the waist. "So, we've got the whole house to ourselves?"

Sam's tense body relaxed into me, and he smiled. "We do. But we've also got a deadline."

"Deadline, shmeadline," I teased, nuzzling into his neck.

He wrapped his arms around me and pulled me close. "I only need about four more hours to finish the site and then a little longer to fix these bugs." He sighed into my hair. "Don't know why I decided to scrap the website and start from nothing."

"It needed it. You said from the beginning that the site needed to be completely rebuilt; it definitely wasn't going to earn us any grants the way it was."

"You're right. Just want it done."

"Mother Nature is throwing a hissy fit. I say we light a fire and get cozy on the couch. Nothing we can do about the power and internet for now."

Sam hugged me close. "You're a good influence on me. Without you, I'd be worrying myself sick over something I can't control—beating myself up for not getting more done before this storm."

"Well, I'm luring you away from work with very strong hints at sex on the couch while a fire blazes, so I'm not sure *good influence* is the right word. But there's nothing we can do about the weather or utilities, so we might as well have a good time while we wait." I wasn't ashamed to admit how excited I was to have an empty house and Sam all to myself.

Having your love interest's teen son around quickly made a person feel like they'd been transported back in time to when they were sneaking around under the watchful eyes of their parents. Except Toby ate a lot more and vacillated between not wanting to shower and running out the hot water when he actually opted to take one.

Even the few times Sam and I had snuck over to my side of the duplex, we'd had to be on constant alert for Toby to come stomping up the steps or slamming through the door.

He was a great kid, and I'd never wish for him to be out of the picture, but there was a completely different vibe in the house when he was away.

And we'd agreed that even though Toby was happy Sam and I were together, we definitely didn't need him traumatized by overhearing us having sex.

So, having a quiet, empty house with no teenager threatening to come pounding up the stairs was like a tiny gift from the sex-with-your-boyfriend gods.

I had every intention of savoring each moment of that gift.

## TEN
### Sam

SEX WITH MATTIE WAS...

Well, the most important part of what Mattie and I had wasn't just about the sex. We had our history, our friendship, the new life we were slowly building together —despite my extreme lack of brain cells and thinking he'd dump me to go after Rafe—and I loved how fully and easily he accepted the role I played in my nephew's life.

Mattie, Toby, and my sister were my entire world.

The fact Mattie had found out about Toby and just rolled with it, taking his place in my nephew's life like it was the most natural next step, meant so much to me.

But sex with Mattie?

That was the pretty paper and gorgeous ribbons wrapping up the world's best gift. I'd scoffed at the idea of mind-blowing sex, but I'd found exactly that when Mattie moved in next door.

Secret and quiet because Toby was next door?

Hot.

Hard and fast because Toby would be home any minute?

Hot.

Video chats while we jerked off from our own beds at night because Toby was in the basement doing homework?

Even hotter.

Having the house to ourselves while our favorite teenager was cozily tucked away from the ice storm at his friend's house?

Hot.

As.

Fuck.

The fire crackled and cast dark shadows throughout the living room. The tree Toby had helped me put together and decorate glowed in its multi-colored-lighted splendor.

And Mattie pulled me close, wrapping me in his arms, and pressing a kiss to the side of my head. We swayed in the silent house, the pelting ice and popping fire providing a bit of background noise. We danced for a moment longer, only our own love song playing in our heads.

When Mattie's lips brushed over mine, his eyes questioning in the firelight as he studied me, nothing else mattered.

Not the ice storm.

Not the power outage.

Not the damn website.

Mattie was all that mattered.

Us. Mattie and me.

And I needed to feel every inch of his skin against mine.

Despite having the entire night to ourselves, we ended up stripped naked and making out on the couch in record time.

I chuckled when Mattie searched the pocket of his jeans and came up with a tiny bottle of lube before he nearly toppled from the couch. "You just carry that around now?" I teased.

Mattie huffed out a laugh. "No, I grabbed it earlier. Whatever we do, we *can't* forget and leave it out here. Toby would absolutely die."

Groaning, I buried my face in his chest. "Pretty sure I would too. I've had the sex talk with him, and so has Tabby, but I don't need my kid knowing anything about my relationship to lube."

"And he definitely doesn't need to know about how his new buddy Mattie plans to absolutely ream his uncle's ass right here in the living room." Mattie's whisper was hot against my ear, and I shivered at the thought of what was to come.

Taking that as his invitation, Mattie pumped lube onto his fingers and slicked them over my hole. "Wanna fuck you 'til I come. Then you can bend me over the couch and ruin me."

His words went straight to my cock, and I rocked my hips, groaning when our rock-hard dicks rutted together. "Fuck, Mattie." With all the blood filling up my cock, my brain decided to short-circuit. "Fuck." Unable to focus on anything but the slide of Mattie's slick fingers in and out of my ass, I whimpered and sucked one of his nipples between my lips.

"Shit, Sam," Mattie hissed. "Get on your knees." Mattie helped me to a kneeling position and moved my arms to lean on the back of the couch. "Don't come when I fuck you." His words were a challenge. "You can't come until you're buried in my ass."

Mattie pressed his cockhead against my hole and entered me slowly, pausing every so often when I tensed at the stinging stretch.

"You good?" he asked when the heat of his throbbing cock threatened to burn me up from the inside out.

Pushing my ass back, begging for his pounding thrusts, I gripped the back of the couch. "Yes. Fuck, Mattie. Yes."

He pulled almost all the way out before slamming back into me, and my cry of pleasure filled the quiet house. Mattie leaned forward, covering my back with his front. "Love you so fucking much," he growled, an arm clutching me tightly to his chest as he fucked me hard and fast. "Gonna fuck you and leave you leaking my cum."

Whimpering, I gripped my cock in hopes of staving off my orgasm. "Yes," I begged. "Give it to me."

Mattie straightened and gripped my hips as he thrust into me over and over. After a final thrust, he paused with a groan as his dick throbbed inside me filling me with his hot load. "Fuck, Sam. Holy fuck."

He pulled from me slowly and kissed me long and deep.

I ended the kiss and reached for the lube. "Stand at the arm of the couch and bend over," I directed as I slicked my cock.

Mattie scrambled to the arm of the couch, his softening cock glistening with lube and cum. Making a show of bending over for me, Mattie pulled his ass cheeks apart. "Don't spend too much time prepping me, I wanna feel the burn."

The orgasm had him spent and pliant, and I worked him open easily. Knowing my own release would come quickly, I pressed my cock against his hole and eased in. "Fuck, Mattie. Look how good you open for me. Look at you stretching for my cock." I drew back and thrust in again, loving the way Mattie cried out and took me deep. "You look so pretty on my dick, Mattie." Mirroring his motions from earlier, I bent down and covered him, wrapping both arms around his chest and squeezing him tight. "I love you," I whispered. "Fuck. God, Mattie. So fuckin' good."

I straightened and dug my fingers into his hips, thinking about the marks I'd leave on his skin.

Mattie whimpered and spread his legs. "Give it to me. Please."

Pistoning my hips, I slammed into him over and over. The tight, slick heat of his hole spurring me on. My balls drawn tight and ready to explode. When Mattie looked over his shoulder with those gorgeous blue eyes and the floppy curls, I lost it. With a growl of pleasure, I paused and poured myself into him. My cock pulsed as my load flooded his hole, and all I could think of was how Mattie was mine. This made him mine. I'd marked him, called him my own.

This was forever.

*We* were forever.

Mattie and Sam.

Easing from him slowly, I helped him stand from his bent position. Snaking my arms around his waist, I held him close and nuzzled at the sensitive spot under his ear. "We should clean up."

"Later," he murmured. "Power's still out. Sleep first."

Making do with quick swipes of tissues, we cleaned the biggest issues before curling together on the couch. With Mattie's chest pressed to my back, I breathed in a deep sigh of contentment.

Sure, the deadline still loomed.

The power was still out.

And I didn't know if we'd get the grant.

But I had my family.

Toby, Tabby, Mattie, and me.

Everything else was just background noise.

Mattie and me.

Toby and Tabitha.

Those were the things that really mattered.

The fire died down as we slept. When we roused, I took care of adding wood to the fire while Mattie put a pot of water on the range.

"Lucky we have a gas stove," he said several minutes later as we dipped washcloths into the warm water and cleaned ourselves up the best we could.

Once we'd assured we wouldn't be glued together with cum in the morning, we used the bathroom, brushed our teeth, and plugged our phones into the portable battery charger.

"How am I so tired?" I failed to stifle a yawn.

"Well, we just fucked each other's brains out," Mattie teased. "Sleep. We both need it. Tomorrow will be a lot of work."

"If the power and internet are back."

"Positive thoughts only. It's Christmas time, we have to believe."

Kissing him thoroughly, I nuzzled my nose against his. "I love you. Thank you for being here and for keeping me grounded."

Mattie shook his head. "I think we ground each other." He curled against my chest and pressed a kiss to my neck. "Love you."

❄

The peppy knock and cheery call of my name from the front door had me jack-knifing awake and Mattie tumbling to the floor.

"Fuck," he mumbled. "Is that Darcy?"

"Yoo-hoo," the voice called again. "Sam, dear? I come with good news. Sam?"

"Shit, shit, shit," I muttered and scrambled for clothes. Yanking on jeans first, I then shoved my head and arms through a t-shirt before helping Mattie to his feet.

"Those are my pants," he said groggily.

"Sorry. I'll see what he wants and send him on his way. Stay here."

Darcy beamed when I opened the door, the bright sunshine already peeking over the horizon. "Good morning, good morning," Darcy started. "Oh dear. Sam, are you okay? You look a mess."

"Um, yeah. Fine. Just been working a lot of long hours. Not getting much sleep."

Mattie popped his head over my shoulder. "Morning, Mayor." His words were sleep rough and oozed with his usual easy-going sex appeal.

Darcy glanced from Mattie to Mattie's door on the other side of the duplex and back again. When the mayor's eyes went wide and traveled up, down, and back up, I had a pretty good idea of what Mattie had come to the door dressed in. Or what he'd come to the door *not* dressed in.

"Oh," Darcy said, his big eyes blinking rapidly. "Oh my. Oh. I see." He gaped for a few moments and then clapped his hands together. "Oh, my word, this is just wonderful. It's like our own Sugar Pine holiday romance. We could be one of those television movies everyone gets so gaga over in the holiday season." He fanned himself. "And to think, I'm the matchmaker."

"You're not really—" I started.

"Mayor," Mattie interrupted. "How can we help you?"

Darcy pressed a hand to his chest. "Oh, yes. Oh dear, where are my manners? I'm so sorry, gentlemen. Just showing up here and interrupting your morning."

"Mayor?" Mattie pressed.

Darcy blinked and shook his head, pulling himself together. "I wanted to let you know I've directed all resources toward your part of town in hopes of getting the power and internet back in service as soon as possible." He held up a hand. "Not that we're not working for the entire town, but I know time is of the essence."

"That would be really helpful," Mattie said.

"Thank you." I shook Darcy's hand.

Somehow, we made it through an awkward goodbye. Darcy headed down the front steps, and I closed the door only to find Mattie in just a pair of briefs and an open flannel shirt.

"You did *not* just come to the door to speak with the mayor in your underwear." I pinched the bridge of my nose. "You know the whole town will know about us by noon."

Mattie grinned. "I don't care. Do you?"

Unable to hide my smile, I shook my head and pulled him into a hug.

"And I didn't come to the door in my underwear," Mattie said.

I pulled back and frowned.

"I came to the door in *your* underwear." He smacked a kiss to my cheek. "And I would have had more clothes if you hadn't run off with my jeans."

"You didn't *have* to come to the door. You nearly gave Darcy a stroke."

"It would have been rude to ignore the mayor," Mattie said, biting his lip to hide a grin.

"How long do you think until the internet is back?" I asked, my hands trailing down and cupping Mattie's ass.

With a groan, he kissed me, our tongues meeting in a slick, hot dance. "It's Christmas Eve Eve so let's hope for a miracle."

"Think we have time?"

"We'll make time," Mattie said as he reached for the buttons on my jeans.

Thirty minutes later, we collapsed in a heap on my bed after fingering, jerking, and sucking each other off. Sweaty, slick, and breathing heavily, all I wanted to do was doze for a few moments.

The front door slammed open.

"Sam? Mattie?" Toby called.

Eyes darting to check the door was locked, I shot up in bed and grabbed a towel.

"Be right there," I yelled as we scrambled from bed and yanked on sweats and t-shirts. "Fuck. Thank god we didn't do that on the couch."

"Thank god we brought the lube with us," Mattie whispered.

We erupted into giggles like teens.

When Toby's footsteps headed toward his room, we grabbed onto the moment like a lifeline and rushed from the bedroom. In the kitchen, we attempted to look busy which, not surprisingly, was hard to do when there was no power.

And we'd nearly gotten caught in a compromising position.

Toby wandered into the kitchen.

"Hey," Mattie said, his voice a bit too high and not nearly as nonchalant as he probably wished it was. "What's up? How was Jasper's? Is the ice melting?" He poured water into the tea kettle and set it on the stove.

Toby eyed him suspiciously. "Jasper's good. The ice is definitely melting."

"Good," I said, trying my best to sound natural. I grabbed mugs and tea bags. "The mayor came by and said we'd hopefully have power and internet back soon."

Toby smirked and rolled his eyes.

"What?" I asked.

"I live with big teenagers who get their freak on every time their kid is out of the house."

Mattie coughed.

I cleared my throat. "We are most definitely not *getting our freak on*," I tried to choke out.

Toby scoffed. "Believe me, it's as painful for me as it is for you."

Mattie busted out in laughter as my nephew left the kitchen with a Christmas cookie.

ELEVEN

*Mattie*

THE POWER CAME BACK on fairly quickly later that day.

The internet, however, held out for much longer.

I headed home for a bit to shower while Sam and Toby did the same at their place. Unsure if I should go back after I'd cleaned up, I puttered around the house for a bit.

Toby knocked on my door, his cheeks pink above a shy smile. "We're going to watch movies if you want to come over."

The three of us piled onto Sam's couch for a Christmas movie screening. Christmas movies in the days leading up to Christmas was something their family had done for a long time, and I got a warm, squishy sensation in my chest when they included me in their tradition.

After a few hours, Sam's anxiety nearly stole the air from the room.

"Why don't we go get some fresh air?" I suggested. "Maybe by the time we get back, the internet will be on."

Toby grumbled a bit, as did Sam, but we pulled on our cold weather gear and headed out for a walk. The day was truly gorgeous. Melting ice provided a soft trickling to the bird song and breeze through the trees. While the day before had been cold enough for an ice storm, the temperature was now well-above freezing, and the sun shone brightly in the sky.

By the time we reached the woods, Toby had stripped his jacket and grabbed a walking stick. We spent an hour or so wandering through the woods and following the river. As a teenager, it was Toby's duty to keep his excitement at bay, but the three of us enjoyed spotting a family of deer drinking at the water's edge.

We also spied the tail of a fox as it scampered away.

And we followed the rat-a-tat-tat of a woodpecker until we found him pecking away at a tree.

Toby exclaimed the bug the woodpecker pulled from the tree was so disgusting, but he tapped out a text to Jasper and sent a photo of the bird's insect lunch.

Despite the hour still being late afternoon, the winter sun had inched low in the sky. Sam seemed less tense, but there was no doubt he was ready to head back when I suggested maybe we turn around.

Toby and I held our breaths and waited as Sam scurried off to his office.

"Yes!" Sam's triumphant cry had Toby and I sighing in relief.

"You want to help me cook dinner so he can work?" I asked Toby.

The kid nodded. "Sure. Probably not getting anything but pizza rolls if I'm counting on him for a meal," he said with a snarky smile.

"He's been working really hard on the website. If we get the grant, Sugar Pine will get a good chunk of money. It's important for the town."

"I know." Toby shrugged and glanced out the window. "Pizza rolls aren't the worst."

"Not the worst, huh?" I elbowed him, and he huffed out a chuckle. The kid could put away a whole bag of pizza rolls in a day.

"What do you want to fix?" Toby asked.

"Figured we could do lasagna or chicken and broccoli casserole." I opened the freezer. "Pretty sure we have everything for both."

"The good lasagna or the scratch kind Sam likes to pretend is the best?" Toby wrinkled his nose.

I couldn't help but laugh. "Some people would pay good money for homemade lasagna as good as Sam's."

"I'd rather pay money for the good ol' frozen kind," Toby said. "If we have the good kind, I want that. I don't really like that casserole."

"Not a fan of broccoli?"

"I love broccoli, I just don't love chicken. I mean, I like it, but we eat a lot of chicken."

"Lasagna it is," I said as I pulled a box from the

freezer. "You're lucky I don't have a single clue how to make it homemade."

Toby and I set to work baking the lasagna and garlic cheese bread.

"We're supposed to have a vegetable," Toby said. "Mom says we should always have a vegetable with dinner."

My heart twinged for the kid. "How about we do an appetizer of carrots and ranch while we wait for this all to bake?"

Toby grabbed a bag of carrots and the bottle of ranch from the fridge. "I'll put a salad on the grocery list."

We took Sam a plate of carrots with a side of ranch. He looked up from his work and blinked as if surprised to see us.

"How's it going?" I asked as Toby peeked over Sam's shoulder at one of the multiple monitors.

"You've got *nestled* spelled wrong." Toby pointed while crunching on a carrot right at his uncle's ear.

Sam closed his eyes and groaned. "About as good as that." He stood and stretched, tiny pops sounding as his spine uncrunched.

"You keep working until dinner," I said. "After dinner, Toby and I will do our best proofreading while you finish up. Bed as usual, no staying up super late to finish. I can already see the headache lines around your eyes. Anything not finished tonight can be finalized tomorrow morning before submitting it."

"I'm good at spotting mistakes," Toby said before heading back to the kitchen.

"I *need* to finish this tonight—"

"You *need* to spend time with your kid. He's on break, he's bored, he's missing his mom. I'll head home, and you guys can watch movies or play video games."

Sam blinked before his eyes skittered away. "Damn, how much do I suck?"

I cocked my head.

"Thank you," he said, pulling me close for a long kiss. "Thank you for reminding me what's really important."

"You don't suck—well, except when it's the fun kind —" I nuzzled my nose against his, heat pooling in my belly when Sam's eyes flamed to life. "You're passionate and dedicated, both really good qualities. Sometimes we just have to remember where certain priorities rank."

"I love you," Sam said, hugging me close.

"Love you too," I whispered.

"And you don't have to head home. Toby adores you. Stay."

I kissed him again. "I'll call you when dinner is ready."

When the oven timer buzzed, Toby and I set the table and poured drinks. Sam's hunger was likely the main reason he came to the kitchen easily. The three of us fell into a comfortable mix of silence and random conversation as we ate.

"Jasper's dad asked if you two are together," Toby said through a mouthful of garlic bread.

My eyes caught Sam's.

"The mayor told someone who told Jasper's dad," Toby said in way of explanation.

"Darcy definitely wasn't gonna keep that to himself," I muttered.

"What did Jasper say?" Sam asked.

"They asked me."

"And what did you say?" Sam pressed.

Toby shrugged. "I said you guys knew each other a long time ago, and it didn't work out, but it was working out now."

This time Sam's eyes caught mine.

"They are, right?" Toby asked. "Working out? That was okay?"

"They're working out just fine," Sam said.

His warm touch on my thigh turned my heart to mush.

"You okay with that?" I asked.

"Sure," Toby said. "I mean, it's whatever." He shrugged as if trying not to care, but he hid a tiny smile behind a bite of lasagna.

As we finished our food and started in on clean-up, Toby's phone buzzed.

"Tell Jasper you'll call back," Sam said.

"It's Mom," Toby said, snatching up his phone. "Mom?" He put the call on speaker. "Say hi to Sam and Mattie."

"Hi, Sam and Mattie." Tabby's voice filled the air, sounding as far away as she truly was. "How's the rental working out, Mattie?"

I couldn't help but grin at the teasing in her words. "It's working out just fine, thank you very much."

Tabby laughed.

"No, really. Thank you," I said. "Not sure our dumb asses would have ever taken the right steps to end up back in each other's lives if it weren't for your scheming."

Tabby laughed again. "Best damn decision ever, signing you as a tenant. Glad you two got things figured out."

Sam and Tabby chatted for a bit about bills, people around town, and future dates for her time at home before Toby took the phone and ran off to his room.

"I swear he somehow manages to get a message to her and have her call right when it's time to do the dishes," Sam grumbled.

"I'll do the dishes every night if it means seeing him so happy to talk to her," I said.

Sam frowned. "Oh, sure, make me look like the grump."

I yanked him close, hugging him to my chest. "Dishes first, then we'll work for a bit. One hour *only*. Then video games if Toby can stand having a couple amateurs playing his game."

Dishes went quickly with two people tackling them, and the three of us soon found ourselves in Sam's office. Toby and I were in charge of different sections of the website as we searched for errors, and Sam finished his list of glitches he wanted to fix.

The timer on my phone went off, and we all groaned. "Time to call it quits for sure. I don't know how you stare at a screen like this all day."

As much as I could tell Sam wanted to keep working on the site, he clicked a few more times and shut everything down. "I say we let Toby smear us in whatever game keeps him so busy these days."

Toby's eyes lit up. "Really? You want to play?" He looked my way. "You're staying?"

"If you want me to," I hedged. Of course, I wanted to stay, but I needed Toby to know I wasn't trying to crowd his space with Sam.

Toby's eyes gleamed, but he shrugged one shoulder. "I mean, you're probably better than Sam, you might as well try to beat me."

We played thirty minutes of a game that reminded me of the Blair Witch movie—the movements on screen and things jumping out had me equal parts dizzy and on-edge.

Toby finally sighed and switched us to Mario Kart.

Neither Sam nor I were much better at the driving game, but at least it was bright and colorful, and we weren't being attacked by zombies.

"How are you guys so bad at this?" Toby asked as he won yet another race. "Didn't they have video games when you were kids?"

Sam elbowed his nephew, and I put the kid in a headlock.

"We had video games, you little brat."

Toby erupted in laughter when I ruffled his hair. He wiggled and squirmed until he escaped my hold.

"We didn't have *these* video games. The controllers are different for one. I haven't played a video game in probably ten or more years."

Toby wrinkled his nose. "What do you *do*? You know, when you're bored?"

"Paint, frame artwork, take photographs, read an art magazine."

Toby nodded. "I get it. I'll probably like old people stuff when I'm your age too."

"Painting isn't *old people stuff*," I said. "It's my job. It's how I make money."

"And he's very good at it," Sam added.

"Well, you both should work on hand-eye-coordination and play some video games from time to time," Toby said as the next race started.

He was halfway down the track before Sam and I even realized the game had started again.

I came awake slowly in the quiet darkness of my bedroom. It was still early on Christmas Eve morning, and Sam was in my bed.

"Did you sneak out of your house?" I murmured into his chest.

We'd finished video games with Toby at a decent hour, and Sam had declared everyone needed a good night's sleep. Toby had disappeared to his room while Sam and I made out like horny teenagers in his kitchen.

Until Toby came down for milk, scolded us for breaking rules, said he'd need bleach for his eyes, and stood with his hands on his hips until I pressed a final kiss to Sam's lips, and ruffled Toby's hair before slipping out the front door.

But now, Sam held me close, his warmth surrounding me, and his soft breathing tickling my cheek.

"I did. Toby will sleep until noon if I let him, but I left a note to tell him where I am in case he wakes early."

"Mmmm, I like waking up with you."

"I finalized everything for the grant and submitted to Darcy about an hour ago. Now we wait." Sam trailed his hand down my bare hip.

"I think everything looks great, we worked hard. *You* were amazing. Even if we don't get the grant, the effort we put into making the site and the town better was worth it."

"Agreed. It needed to be done, and it will benefit the town in the future." Sam pressed a kiss to the top of my head. "Just remind me never to take a deadline so near to the holidays."

We dozed for a while, enjoying the lazy closeness.

"Are we going to see the gingerbread house display?" I asked later, my words sleepy as the sun began to peek through the windows.

"We are," Sam mumbled. "Toby wants to go grab brunch first, then we'll head over to the community center. I think *a lot* of people entered the contest."

"So, we have some time?"

Sam chuckled as my words registered. Then he groaned and sucked on my earlobe. "Plenty of time."

Christmas Eve sex with the man I planned to spend the rest of my life with turned out to be slow and gentle as we rocked each other's worlds. Afterward, we lay tangled together, sweat and cum cooling on our skin while we caught our breaths, and I knew without a shadow of a doubt that my future was mapped out with Sam in Sugar Pine.

I hadn't come to town with Christmas wishes and hopes of a forever love, but that was exactly what I'd found.

Our phones buzzed.

Toby: Gross. Hurry up. Let's go eat.

Sam groaned.

I laughed.

We rolled from bed and jumped into the shower.

Thirty minutes later, Toby rolled his eyes at us as he threw on his hoodie.

"It's cold out," Sam warned.

"I'm good," Toby muttered.

Sam started to argue, but I caught his eye and shook my head.

Toby headed down the front steps.

"It's freezing out here," Sam complained.

"I saw a thread on the single dads' forum about preteens and teens. Hoodies, all the time. Just a hoodie in the cold, and still wearing it when it's hot. There was a lot of talk regarding the psychology of it all, but basically, it's normal. We're just going to the diner and community center, so it's not like he'll freeze to death. Don't fight it. The forum dads actually said the more parents fight it, the more the teens often dig in their heels."

Sam huffed and rolled his eyes, but kept his mouth shut as we followed Toby down the steps.

Our first stop was the little diner for brunch. They'd gone all out with the gingerbread theme. Gingerbread pancakes, gingerbread French toast, gingerbread chai latte and dark roast from One Lump or Two, and a gingerbread cinnamon roll. The brunch menu also included sugar plum treats from the bakery in the form of tarts, crumble, and coffee cake.

Toby's face lit up mid-meal when his phone buzzed. "Can I hang out with Jasper at the gingerbread thing?"

Sam nodded. "As long as you two stay in the community center and remember your manners."

Toby agreed and spent the rest of the meal chatting about the various people he knew who had entered the contest. Amazing what the promise of time with a friend could do for a person.

We paid the bill and headed out into the cold, crisp Christmas Eve morning. Luckily, the sun was warm. We most likely wouldn't see a single snowflake for Christmas this year, but the sun was a decent trade off.

The Gingerbread House Extravaganza turned out to be bigger and better than the three of us had originally imagined.

"And they're going to make it bigger next year?" Sam asked in awe.

"We'll have to think about entering a category," I said. "Let's pick one today; we'll need a year to plan."

"As the brains behind the whole thing, we shouldn't be allowed to win," Toby said. "But maybe we can enter in the Family Fun category."

My heart warmed at the look of love and pride filling Sam's face as he watched his nephew. Toby shrugged and muttered, "What?" before looking at his phone.

A few moments later, Jasper found us near the entrance and gave a quick hello before Toby dragged them off in search of gingerbread hot chocolate and the winning entry.

As Sam and I wandered the exhibits and took in the different entries for each category, we decided that Sugar Pine, and the surrounding towns, had a vast amount of talent.

"Just think, this is what came together with very little

time to plan. Can't imagine how much folks will expand their creativity next year."

Toby and Jasper met us in one of the rows and declared they'd found the overall winner for sure. But they also walked with us for a bit, and pointed out the houses they thought should win their categories.

We ran into Darcy and let him introduce us to some folks as he bustled about and gushed about all the amazing things Sugar Pine had to offer. When we finally made our excuses and cut away from the mayor, Toby asked if we could just get food at the event rather than going home to cook.

"I'm good with no dishes," Sam said.

We ate and laughed, visited with Sugar Pine residents old and new, and enjoyed our Christmas Eve outing both as a couple and a family of three—even though we were sadly missing our fourth.

Toby didn't mention his mom, but there was a bittersweet catch in his voice when he took her call later that night. He ran off to his room to talk, catching Tabby up on all the happenings, and celebrating Christmas Eve with her from a thousand miles away.

"You wanna come over tomorrow morning?" Sam asked as he walked me to my door.

Yes.

Yes, I wanted to spend Christmas morning with Sam and Toby.

But...

"I don't want to intrude."

"You're not intruding. Toby likes you more than he likes me most of the time. He'd be glad to have you there." Sam pressed kisses along my jawline.

I groaned, wrapping my arms around his waist. "Let's play it by ear. If he asks for me, I'll gladly be there. If he doesn't, you two just enjoy your Christmas morning together, and I can come over later." I brushed a kiss over his lips. "You don't have many more Christmases with him home, take advantage of them."

"God," Sam groused. "Why don't you just stab me in the heart? *We* don't have many more Christmases with him home. But I get what you're saying. I'll see how he wants it to play out. Either way, you're coming over at some point. I'm not spending Christmas Day apart if I don't have to."

"Sleep tight. Maybe Santa will bring you everything you wanted." The kiss was longer, slower, and hotter this time.

"I already have everything I want," Sam whispered against my lips. "I love you, Mattie. I get not wanting to overwhelm Toby, but this isn't just a fling. You're part of our family, and I want to share the moment with you."

"I love you," I said, nuzzling his nose. "Just see how Toby wants to play it. He's already missing his mom; I don't want to trample all over his Christmas morning."

"Okay, we'll see. But be prepared for an early wake-up." Sam kissed me, slapped me on the ass, and headed toward his side of the duplex.

"Wait, what? How early?"

The love of my life, the man I'd fallen for way back then, and found again for our very own second chance at forever, just laughed.

## TWELVE

### Sam

ONE OF THESE CHRISTMAS MORNINGS, Toby jumping on my bed to wake me up at the ass crack of dawn was going to scare me so badly I'd have a heart attack.

My early demise would really put a damper on Christmas.

*One year, much too soon, there will be no Toby jumping on your bed to wake you up at all. He'll want to sleep later. Or he'll be off at school. Or the military. Or waking up with his own little family.*

Well, with that cheery little thought clogging my throat and stinging my eyes, I groaned and played the game Toby and I had been playing since he was tiny.

I pretended to be asleep.

Toby hit me with a pillow.

I said I didn't want to go to work today.

He reminded me it was Christmas.

I said Santa could wait.

He begged and pleaded.

I finally growled, put him in a headlock, and ruffled his hair while he howled and kicked those long, gangly teen boy legs. Then I rolled out of bed and tried not to grimace at the red numbers glowing on the bedside clock.

With a grin, I imagined Mattie's horror at being awakened at such an early hour. He was an artist. He kept his own hours, but those most definitely didn't include anything before six in the morning.

And yet, here we were.

"Is Mattie awake? He's coming, right?" Toby asked excitedly as I stumbled from the bathroom a few moments later to start coffee.

Maybe knowing Toby wanted him with us on Christmas morning would help ease the pain of being dragged from bed at 4:45 a.m. "You wanna go wake him up? Give him the Toby-fied version of Christmas morning?"

The kid's eyes gleamed, and he nodded. How was he so damn awake?

Damn, I was going to miss this.

Back when he was a toddler, a child, even a tween, it seemed like we had all the time in the world. It was easy to bellyache about the ungodly wakeup time because we had more years to look forward to.

We still had the years to look forward to, but they

were different. The Christmas mornings ahead were full of changes. Promises of being so proud of the young adult Toby was becoming, yet heartache at what we'd left behind.

Watching him tackle the world while wishing for one more Christmas morning together as my five-year-old tore into his gifts or demolished powdered donuts in front of a final viewing of Frosty the Snowman for the season.

In the years to come, our family would trade old traditions for new ones. I was grateful these changes happened slowly over the years because my chest already ached as if I'd been run over by a train.

Parenting—and maybe life in general—was full of celebrating new milestones, mourning what we'd left behind, and looking forward to that next stage. It was the way life worked. There were parts of the past I was grateful to be done with, but there were days when I'd give anything to cuddle Toby as a baby, push him on a swing as a toddler, let him fall asleep on my shoulder, or tuck him into bed.

The front door opened, and Mattie stumbled in after Toby looking as if he'd been dragged from bed in the middle of the night by a crazed intruder.

Well, he wasn't far off...

Mattie's gorgeous hair was a mess; he'd had no time to coerce it into its usual perfection. His eyes sleepy, but curious. Flannel pajama pants slung low on his hips, a fitted t-shirt clung to him just right, and a smirk on those pretty pink lips completed the look.

"Good morning," I whispered when Mattie made his way to the kitchen and leaned in for a kiss. "Coffee?"

"Dear God in Heaven, Baby Jesus, Santa, and Frosty all rolled into one, yes." Desperation laced his words, but his eyes sparkled. Despite being awakened at a very rude hour, Mattie was excited for Christmas.

With his family.

Toby groaned. "Oh my god, please keep it in your pants. Let's go. You two can make out later." He bounced from one side to the other, his hoodie strings swaying.

Still my little boy in that lanky body. Stuck, for the moment, between childhood and adulthood. But on Christmas morning, the childhood side won out.

Mattie and I quickly doctored our coffees before following Toby to the living room. After a long fortifying sip of his coffee, Mattie got the fire going while Toby passed out gifts. I texted Tabby to let her know we were opening gifts, but I knew the time difference and her assignments didn't always allow her to drop everything and make a call. I promised to video everything to share with her later in case she couldn't call right away.

Toby made some sort of *wait a minute* sound and ran off toward his room.

Mattie settled next to me on the couch and slurped down more coffee. "Thanks for inviting me," he whispered.

"It wasn't me. Toby asked. I told you to be ready for early; guess I should have suggested you lock your door." I bumped his shoulder with mine.

"I had no idea. Even if you'd told me a time, I wouldn't have been prepared." He spoke like a man who'd experienced something out-of-this-world. "So much energy. I nearly pissed myself when he jumped on my bed."

I laughed and stretched my arm around Mattie's shoulders to pull him close. "He's been doing that since he could walk and understood that Christmas morning meant gifts."

"It's sweet. And even though it's a shock to the system, I imagine there will be Christmas mornings in the future when we'll miss it." He pressed a kiss to my cheek as I blinked stinging eyes.

"Yeah," I managed to choke out. "Things are changing. I mean, they're always changing, but these seem like bigger changes looming ahead."

"He's a great kid. You've done an amazing job with him. Changes are going to happen whether we're ready or not, but even the hard ones can bring good things." He rested his forehead against my temple. "I love you. We'll tackle the future together."

"Promise?" The catch in my throat caught the word and mangled it a bit.

"As long as you'll have me."

Toby returned with great gusto and handed us each a gorgeously wrapped gift box. "Jasper's mom wrapped them for me. I tried, but my wrapping skills are about the same as your video game skills."

We let Toby open a couple gifts first. He liked the new hoodie, jeans, and shoes, but I knew he was really hoping for a certain video game in one of the next boxes.

My gift to Mattie wasn't super romantic, but hopefully practical and appreciated. I built a new website for him. Yeah, he had one, but this one would have all the bells and whistles. I'd worked slowly on it due to the deadline, but Mattie could help me with making sure the finishing touches were to his liking, and we'd have it up and running for selling his artwork by the first of the year.

"Thank you," Mattie said, running his hand over the piece of paper describing his gift. "I went with cheap and easy to have an online presence, but this is amazing."

Mattie's gift for me blew the website out of the water. He'd painted and framed multiple pieces. One of him and me; it was gorgeous, and I knew exactly where I'd hang it.

He'd also done a beautiful painting of Toby and Tabby from the last time she was home. All three of us got one of those.

And Toby even seemed touched to see the framed painting of him and Jasper.

"Thought you could put it on your wall," Mattie said with a shrug, as if his artwork wasn't an absolute splendor.

Toby snapped a picture of the painting and tapped

out a text, most likely sending it to Jasper right then. Hopefully his friend was also an early riser on Christmas morning.

My smartass nephew gave me a pair of reading glasses.

"So you don't have to hold papers so far away."

He also gifted me with five coupons for doing the dishes.

I waved them in his face. "Do these come with a guarantee of not having to ask you a thousand times?"

Toby scoffed. "I always end up doing them." Then he smirked. "Maybe just not right when you want them done."

Then he handed me a plastic baggie of coupons cut from mailers.

Coupons for frozen lasagna.

"A dollar off the good kind." Toby grinned. "You can fix your homemade kind when you're trying to be all romantic and shit."

"I'll fix the *good* kind for Mattie and me; you can have cereal."

It was Toby's turn to open another gift. He picked the box with some gaming accessories. He said thanks, but his eyes lingered longingly on the next to last box.

Mattie buzzed with anticipation next to me, and I knew he was as excited about Toby opening that game as the kid was.

Mattie and I opened the festively wrapped gifts from Toby next.

And Christmas morning stood still.

The only movement in the room was the shifting of logs in the fire, my heart melting, and Mattie taking my hand.

"Toby." Mattie's words caught in his throat. "Thank you."

Toby shrugged. "Just thought you guys should know. I'm good with it. *Really* good."

My eyes stung as Mattie and I stared at the matching picture frames resting on our knees. The photo in both was one of the three of us we'd taken one day not long ago. But the frame was what really tugged on my heartstrings.

Maybe even more so for Mattie.

The simple wooden frame complimented the photograph perfectly.

And the word *Dad* adorned the bottom right corner.

Toby's love and acceptance—of me, of what I'd found with Mattie, of our unique little family—was the most precious gift I'd received since the day they placed him in my arms all wrapped up in the hospital blanket.

"Thank you. This is beautiful, and it means a lot." I blinked back the tears. "Go ahead," I said with a chuckle. "Open your last ones."

Toby tore into the box and whooped when he discovered the coveted video game. Just when I knew he wanted to rush to the basement and start playing, I nodded toward the card.

"What's this?" Toby asked. He opened the card and read. "For real?"

I nodded, and the next thing I knew I had an armful of teenager as he hugged first me and then Mattie. "This is the best. When can we do it? Tomorrow?"

I laughed. "How about you check with your friends and see when they're available. Let's do it Saturday maybe if that works for everyone. That gives us time to buy snacks."

Toby nodded and clutched the game and new controller to his chest as he made his way toward the basement door. "Thank you!" he called out as he rumbled down the stairs.

"Think we'll survive four teens gorging themselves on snacks and playing video games all night?" Mattie asked as he rested his head on my shoulder.

"I'm just glad he seems happy. The years Tabby isn't here at Christmas are always hard. If a sleepover can keep him distracted from missing her, I'm all for it."

Warm and toasty in front of the fire, I tugged Mattie down to cuddle on the couch with me. The sun wasn't even up yet; anything we needed to do could wait until we napped.

"Merry Christmas." Mattie's sleepy words feathered over my lips. "I love you."

"Love you," I murmured. "Merry Christmas."

A couple hours later, Mattie's kisses to my neck woke me. The living room glowed with Christmas lights and bright sunshine. Groaning and reveling in the press of our bodies, I tipped his face up and captured his mouth. Savoring the flavor of him on my tongue, we kissed for several long moments before dozing for a few more minutes.

"Probably need to check on Toby and figure out what's for breakfast," I mumbled a bit later.

We unfolded ourselves from the comfy couch, used the bathroom, and gathered up the discarded wrapping paper. With new mugs of coffee in hand, we made our way to the basement door.

The basement was suspiciously quiet, and we found Toby passed out on his bean bag with a controller in hand and his new video game softly playing music on the screen.

"Some of the dads on the forum would probably tell me to wake him up so we don't mess up his sleep schedule," I said.

"But?"

I shrugged. "But it's Christmas. I think it's fine. He'll wake when he wakes. Let him be a kid." I took the controller from Toby's hand and placed a blanket over him while Mattie turned off the game.

Once we were back upstairs, Mattie took me in his arms and hugged me tight. "Will you need to leave the forum?"

"Why would I leave the forum?"

Mattie smirked. "You're not a single dad anymore."

I started to protest, but then his words sank in, and

all I could do was smile. "I guess I'm not, am I? Maybe they'll let me stick around."

"If not, we'll figure out these teen years together." He led me to the couch and settled with me tucked under his arm.

"Are you sure you want to stay here?" My heart suddenly clenched at the thought I was clipping his wings.

"Do you not want me here?"

"No, it's not that. But I have at least four or five more years before I can even think of taking off." The thought of leaving Sugar Pine hurt my stomach.

"I ran from here because I needed to figure myself out. I know why things didn't work in California. My roots are here, and this is where I want to be. With you. This is my home." Mattie kissed me gently, his fingers playing with the hair at the nape of my neck. "Maybe when Tabby's home we can think of some short trips. Just us or all four of us."

"I don't want to hold you back," I hedged.

"You're not. Coming back here was the best decision I ever made. We got a second chance, and I don't want to waste that."

With the fire smoldering, and the peacefulness of Christmas cloaking the room, I clinked my coffee cup against Mattie's. "To second chances and many more Christmases to come."

"Second chances and Sugar Pine Christmases."

Mattie bumped his mug to mine. "Definitely my very own Christmas wish come true."

My phone buzzed on the coffee table.

"Ignore it," Mattie urged.

"It might be Tabby." I grabbed my phone.

"Who is it?"

"Darcy," I said. Thumbing the screen, I accepted the call.

## Epilogue

MATTIE

### *Two and a Half Years Later*

The summer sun shone through the window catching dust motes floating on the air. The scent of Mattie's shampoo teased my nose, and I pressed a kiss to the back of his neck in a sleepy haze.

My phone buzzed on the bedside table.

The first day of summer vacation for Toby looked to be dawning bright and clear. No doubt, he'd be itching to go to Jasper's and spend the day doing whatever the two of them did.

Jasper was a good kid, and they had been a loyal support for Toby over the years. My nephew hadn't outright *said* he had a thing for Jasper, but I'd noticed a bit of a change in their interactions over the last couple years.

As long as Toby was safe and happy, I had no qualms

over who he fell for. Mattie and I had fun watching the little love story play out.

My phone buzzed again.

Mattie hadn't turned on the air conditioning in his side of the duplex just yet, and a soft breeze fluttered the curtains in his bedroom. I knew I needed to check my texts, but I wasn't above ignoring them for a few more moments.

Tabby was home for a surprise two-week stay before she went back to finish this round of deployment. Toby had been ecstatic to see her sitting on the front porch when he got home from school a few days ago. They'd pretty much been inseparable since, but Tabby had to drive to the base today, and I knew Toby would take advantage of the guilt-free freedom to hang with his friend.

My phone buzzed.

Again.

Mattie, Darcy, and I were meeting today to go over plans for the Sugar Pine Gingerbread House Extravaganza. It had nearly tripled in size since the inaugural year.

Darcy had been so thrilled when he called on that Christmas morning two years ago to let us know we'd gotten the grant. And he'd nearly combusted when he found out we'd gotten a three-year extension on the grant. Tourism was way up, and Sugar Pine was back in the black. We were now known for the gingerbread house competition and festival. People came from all over to enter for prizes and view the amazing talents on display.

When my phone buzzed two more times, I finally admitted defeat and grabbed it from the nightstand.

"Who is it?" Mattie curled into my side and threw his leg over mine, a hand caressing down my torso.

> Tabby: Get your asses out of bed. You can boink later. I have coffee.

> Toby: Mom said I can go to Jasper's. We're going to hike the woods today. They want to take a picnic. Can I borrow your gas card?

"You sure you want to be part of this crazy life?" I asked as we chuckled over the texts.

Mattie pulled me close. "Even if I didn't, I'm way too invested now. We've got a unique setup, but it works for us."

"Well, I guess we better get going. Coffee sounds good, and we slept later than Toby, so it's definitely time to get up."

"We can boink later," Mattie teased.

After quickly washing our faces and brushing our teeth, we pulled on clothes and made our way to the front porch. Toby and his mom sat on the swing. Tabby sipped her coffee, her uniform crisp and hair pulled back in a tight bun. Toby flicked his keychain as he told her some funny story about the last day of school.

I produced my gas card and handed it to my nephew.

He and Jasper had jobs lined up for the summer, but Tabby and I had agreed to help him with gas as needed. He was a good, responsible driver, and he didn't go far— mainly just driving in and around Sugar Pine—so we didn't mind helping.

"Thanks," Toby said with a grin. He hugged his mom. "See you tonight. Movie tomorrow?"

I loved that they were getting time together. All of Tabby's deployments had been challenges, some more than others, but Toby had really been missing her this time around. Having her come home for a two-week surprise had been just what he needed to start his summer break.

He ran down the steps and climbed into the car we'd got him. It wasn't new, it wasn't shiny, and it didn't run like a dream. But it was solid, got good gas mileage, and was a good vehicle for a first-time driver. Toby and Mattie had taken to pulling the car into the yard and tinkering on it a couple evenings and weekends lately. Those two were thick as thieves, and I loved seeing their relationship grow. They were good for each other. Thanks to our unique setup, Mattie kinda took over the uncle position I couldn't fill because of stepping into the dad position.

The three of us stood on the porch and watched Toby drive away. Tabby's head on my shoulder, Mattie's hand in mine. When Tabby got home for her long stretch in a few months, Mattie and I would head out for a week-long trip out west. Over Christmas break, the four of us were going to Florida to visit Disney World.

But until then, we had a couple weeks to enjoy as a family of four.

Maybe we weren't the *normal* family unit, but it was our normal, and I loved the little life we'd built.

~THE END~

Don't miss the other Single Dads All the Way titles:
A Kickin' Karate Christmas by Essie Sloane
A Candy Cane Christmas by Ray Celar
A Magically Delicious Christmas by AE Madsen
A Merry Penthouse Christmas by Amanda Meuwissen

Want more addictive, sexy, emotional M/M romance?
Check out all of A.D. Ellis's books on Amazon.
Want to immediately fall in love with more holiday stories?
Run, do not walk, to Peppermint Hollow and dive right in to all the steamy, swoony M/M holiday goodness.
Or find even more M/M holiday stories on my direct store HERE.
Sign up for the A.D. Ellis newsletter so you never miss a new release or sale.
https://www.subscribepage.com/
ADEllisNewsMMRomance

Also by A. D. Ellis

Want more Christmas? Look no further!

A Touch of Christmas Magic - Come back to Peppermint Hollow and visit with Ivy and Em! **_A Touch of Christmas Magic_ is a steamy M/M romance between two completely oblivious best friends featuring first-time parenting, a bisexual awakening, and found-family all wrapped up in a feel-good holiday love story. **

Holly Hills Christmas- **Holly Hills Christmas** is a steamy, feel-good, M/M age-gap holiday romance.

Listen to Your Heart- **Listen to Your Heart** is a steamy, second chance, M/M romance with just enough holiday magic to make you believe. It shares the same world with **Follow Your Heart** by Declan Rhodes.

The Heart of St. Nick- _The Heart of St. Nick is a steamy, forced proximity, small-town M/M holiday romance with a slight age gap between a bowtie and suspender-wearing good guy and an emotionally-stunted man with a cold heart just waiting to be melted._

Peaches & Cream: The Men of Haven Grove - _a steamy, age-gap, friends-to-lovers M/M romance between a jack-of-all-trades and his dad's best friend._

Two Weeks in Paradise- an opposites-attract, forced proximity M/M romance between two widowers nearing fifty. This low-angst love story is perfect for fans of kinky steam mixed with sweet fluff.

Jett & Leighton: On Cravenwood Block- a steamy, opposites-attract, bisexual-awakening, roommates-to-lovers M/M romance featuring a sexy-as-sin tattoo artist and a fresh, flashy barista with a smile that lights up the room.

Silver in the City (3 books- meet the Silver crew you read about in Forged in the City) Available on AUDIO!

Forged in the City (3 books- a spin-off series from Silver in the City) Available on AUDIO

The BJ Boys Series (3 books, small town, big love) Available on AUDIO

Forever Better Together (friends to lovers) Available on AUDIO!

His Reluctant Cowboy (age gap, opposites attract, cowboy romance) Available on AUDIO!

What Blooms Beneath (LGBT Fantasy romance) Available on AUDIO!

# About the Author

A.D. Ellis is an Indiana girl, born and raised. She spends much of her time in central Indiana as an instructional coach/teacher in the inner city of Indianapolis, being a mom to two amazing older teenagers, and wondering how she and her husband of over two decades haven't driven each other insane yet. A lot of her time is also devoted to phone call avoidance and her hatred of cooking.

She loves chocolate, wine, pizza, and naps along with reading and writing romance. These loves don't leave much time for housework. Who would pick cleaning the house over a nap or a good book? She uses any extra time to increase her fluency in sarcasm.

A.D. uses she/they pronouns.

Website http://adellisauthor.com/

Find me EVERYWHERE at https://www.adellisauthor.com/mylinks/

# Connect with A.D. Ellis

Follow my website http://www.adellisauthor.com or find me on Facebook

http://www.facebook.com/adellisauthor

If you want to get updates about releases, interviews, sales, giveaways, and more please sign up for my newsletter http://www.subscribepage.com/ADEllisNewsMM Romance

Find me on Spotify if you'd like to listen to the playlist for this book (mainly just the songs I listened to while writing). Just search for A.D. Ellis.

To make it easy, find me EVERYWHERE here- https://www.adellisauthor.com/mylinks/

# Acknowledgments

It's always so hard to write this part because I'm worried I'll forget someone without meaning to.

Big thanks to the authors in this collaboration with me!

Readers- you are the reason I write. As long as you continue reading my stories, I'll continue writing them. Thank you for your support.

Bloggers- your support, reviews, and promotion are very much appreciated. Thank you!

My author buddies- I don't know that I could keep doing this without our brainstorm sessions, laughter, road trips, meals, wine, and friendship as my support.

Thank you to my alpha readers, betas, editors, proof-readers, and ARC readers! Your eyes and input are beyond important to me.

Brett and Gage- as usual, I doubt you even grasp how much your support, input, and friendship mean to me. This author journey has brought many wonderful things into my life, and you both are two of the BEST! I'm blessed to call you friends.

My family and friends- thank you for your love and support, always.